A Certain Retribution

Books by Michael Lister

(John Jordan Novels)
Power in the Blood
Blood of the Lamb
Flesh and Blood
The Body and the Blood
Blood Sacrifice
Rivers to Blood
Innocent Blood
Blood Money

(Jimmy "Soldier" Riley Novels)
The Big Goodbye
The Big Beyond
The Big Hello
In a Spider's Web

(Merrick McKnight / Reggie Summers Novels)
Thunder Beach
A Certain Retribution

(Remington James Novels)
Double Exposure
Separation Anxiety

(Sam Michaels / Daniel Davis Novels)
Burnt Offerings
Separation Anxiety

(Love Stories)
Carrie's Gift

(Short Story Collections)
North Florida Noir
Florida Heat Wave
Delta Blues
Another Quiet Night in Desparation

(The Meaning Series)
The Meaning of Jesus
Meaning Every Moment
The Meaning of Life in Movies

Sign up for Michael's newsletter at
www.MichaelLister.com and receive a free book.

A Certain Retribution
Michael Lister

a Merrick McKnight novel
introducing Reggie Summers

Pulpwood Press

You buy a book. We plant a tree.

Copyright © 2014 by Michael Lister

All rights reserved. No part of this book may be reproduced in any form or by any means, electronic or mechanical, including photocopying, recording, or by any information storage and retrieval system, without permission in writing from the publisher.

This is a work of fiction. Any similarities to people or places, living or dead, is purely coincidental.

Inquiries should be addressed to:
Pulpwood Press
P.O. Box 35038
Panama City, FL 32412

Lister, Michael.
A Certain Retribution/ Michael Lister.
-----1st ed.
p. cm.

ISBN: 978-1-888146-45-5 Hardcover

ISBN: 978-1-888146-46-2 Paperback

Library of Congress Control Number:

Book Design by Adam Ake

Printed in the United States

1 3 5 7 9 10 8 6 4 2

First Edition

For My Reggie

Dawn, my inspiration, my partner, my everything.

Thank you

Dawn Lister, Jill Mueller, Adam Ake, Amy Moore-Benson, Micah Lister, Meleah Lister, Travis Roberson, Mike Lister, Judi Lister, Lynn Wallace, Mike Harrison, Tony Justice, Emily Balazs, Tony Simmons, Tim Croft, and Dr. D. P. Lyle

I see her for the first time in over twenty years the night before she'll be arrested.

We have both stopped by the Tiki Grill for takeout—her for her sixteen-year-old son who has just finished football practice, me just for me. Casey has taken Kevin to the fair in Panama City and I am on my own for the evening.

—You don't remember me, do you? she says.

She is a few years younger than me, which back in high school was an eternity, but we had hung out some and had even gone on an ill-fated date.

We had both grown up in Wewathitchka, a small North Florida town of a few thousand people. Wewa to locals. We had both gone to Wewa High. Both moved away. I had moved back to the town famous for tupelo honey and the Dead Lakes a long time ago now, where for four generations my family had owned and operated the weekly newspaper and produced commercial grade tupelo honey, but it's the first time I've seen her since school.

—Of course I do, I say, thinking I could never forget those eyes. Those beyond striking, beyond beautiful, beyond mesmerizing blue-green-gray eyes.

Though there are two tiny tables, the Tiki Grill is mostly a carryout joint. Thankfully we're the only two people in the place. We stand not far from the counter, but drift farther and farther back from it as we talk.

—You do? she says, genuinely surprised, and I find it altogether endearing.

—Reggie Summers, I say so she really knows I know.

She has straight, longish saddle-brown hair and a natural river-clay skin tone most models would die for. She is unassuming and kind of shy—or is it insecure? Whatever it is, everything about her is authentic.

When a beautiful woman doesn't assume you remember her, when she's truly pleased that you do, it's as refreshing as a cool autumnal breeze on a North Florida fall night.

—How are you? I say. You look good.

Only a few inches shorter than me, her powerful five-nine frame is muscular and sturdy and looks like the body of an aging athlete. She's in tightish jeans that show off the amazing ass of her nice full figure, a brown, hooded zipped-up sports jacket, and a pair of well-worn gypsy round-toe cowgirl boots with a roper heel and short pink camo shaft. The topstitching in the brown leather of her boots reminds me of saddles, and I recall just how much she used to ride.

—You too, she says. And I'm okay.

There's more there and I wonder if I should ask.

—Merrick McKnight, she says shaking her head. Can't believe you remember me. What about you? How are you?

—I'm actually pretty good, I say. Considering.

—Considering?

—I just meant . . .

—You could tell me what you really meant, she says.

I smile. She's making me do that a lot.

—I could, couldn't I?

I'm already enjoying this brief conversation more than any I've had in . . . months. Maybe longer. Maybe a lot longer.

—I meant . . . you know how life is. Nothin's turned out the way I expected. Had some pretty horrible shit happen. Not much in my world that says I should be, but I'm pretty damn happy.

She looks and nods in a way that lets me know she knows about Monica and Ty.

—I was so sorry to hear about . . . about what happened

A Certain Retribution

. . . to your wife and son. I mean I assume that's what you're talking about. Horrible shit doesn't get much horribler than that.

I nod.

—It's been a long time ago now. Sometimes I go an entire hour without thinking about it.

—Sorry, she says, shaking her head. It's just so . . .

—What about you? I say.

—Same.

—Which part?

—All but the pretty damn happy part, she says with a smile. You'll have to teach me the trick to that one sometime.

—How about tonight? I say before I realize what I'm saying.

—Huh?

—Sorry. That just shot out.

—Well you can't take it back now. What'd you have in mind?

—We could carry our food next door to Tucks and—

The Tiki Grill is in a small building that is joined by a partially covered courtyard to a bigger building that houses a bar named Tukedawayz Tavern. Both places are operated by our mutual friends Peach and Stacy and mostly function as one establishment.

—Sounds nice, she says. But I can't right now. Have to get my kid home and fed and bathed and to bed.

I nod.

I'm disappointed and a little embarrassed for asking so quickly, but try not to show it.

—Some other time, I say.

—I might be able to get out for a little while after that, she says. We could meet for a beer. Can you tell me the secret to a happy life over a Bud Light?

—That's the best way. You know what Houseman said. *Malt does more than Milton can to justify the ways of God to man.*

She smiles.

—I like that. Can't promise I can get back out, but I'll really try.

She leaves without giving me her number, and I know I'll spend the rest of the night waiting in the bar just for the chance to talk to her some more.

She drives away in her small truck thinking about what just happened.

Did Merrick McKnight just show interest in me? Sure seemed to.

There's no way to get everything done and go back out to the bar, is there?

Beside her, Rain, her sixteen-year-old son, in his sweaty, smelly football pants and jersey, prattles on about practice and his first day at the school she had gone to when she was his age, but only the occasional bit breaks through.

She has so much to do and tomorrow is such a big day. Still, Merrick McKnight.

He's not interested in your certified country bumpkin ass. He was just being polite. No way he'd go for a broke-ass, white trash, single mom, college dropout like you.

—I think I may even start this Friday night, Rain is saying. Offense and defense.

Have to check on Mom. Make sure she is okay. Make sure Rain does his homework. Unpack enough shit to at least be able to brush our teeth and have something to wear tomorrow. Prepare for the meeting.

She's so tired already.

It's a bad idea. Spend some time with your files and then go to bed instead.

—You know what I'm sayin'? Rain asks.

She nods.

—I mean I wouldn't want some new kid coming in and taking my spot either, but if he's better . . . you know what I'm sayin'?

—You can go ahead and eat, she says. Don't have to wait till we get to Grandma's.

A Certain Retribution

—You serious?

—It'll save time. See if you can finish before we get there.

Gonna give your kid indigestion just so you can go back and see if Merrick really was checking out your ass.

—I don't mean to rush, she says. Just . . . it'll take us a few minutes to get there.

—I'm starving. It'll be gone before we get to the dam. Know what I'm sayin'?

Speeding down the twisting road that snakes toward the river, cypresses and pines in the soft glow of sunset on either side, she realizes just how much she's missed this place. It's so beautiful, and it's home no matter how haunted for her it may be.

Time to exorcise some demons, maybe even make a few people pay.

Maybe? Maybe? It's why you're here and you know it.

Part of why I'm here. Only part.

You're no longer that scared little seventeen-year-old victim, so don't act like it. Stay away from the bar. Probably best not to fuck this up before it even begins.

Instead of going straight over to Tucks, I decide to ride around town while I eat my dinner and try to think of someone I can get to go back out to the bar with me tonight.

As I drive around I'm reminded again of just how much I love this place.

Legend has it that the name Wewahitchka originated from an unknown Indian language and means *water eyes*, because of the two nearly perfectly round lakes in the center of town. They are named Alice and Julia, after the daughters of one of the area's earliest settlers, according to local lore.

Wewa is a wild, untamed region—backwoods, dirt roads, untouched, unspoiled, in some ways unwelcoming. Not unwelcoming enough to outsiders, for those of us who call it home. I love it like only a native can, and I have no intention of ever living anywhere else.

Amid seemingly endless rows of slash pines, its flat land is lined with dirt roads covered by oak tree canopies, Spanish moss draped over their branches, blowing like a lace curtain in a summer breeze.

This brutally beautiful place is home to the legendary Dead Lakes, a hauntingly breathtaking body of water that serves as graveyard to thousands of bottom-heavy cypress skeletons, stumps, and knees. It is said that the lake was formed when the Apalachicola's current created sandbars that blocked the Chipola River, causing the high water that killed the trees.

Wewahitchka was birthed by the transportation waterways of the Apalachicola and Chipola rivers and has been in limbo ever since rural roads became the primary transit routes. Will Wewa go the way of Iola, a small river town that no longer exists? Iola, just a few short miles away, was integral in the 1800s as the northern terminus of the busy St. Joseph and Iola Railroad—but now there is no trace the town ever existed. Or will Wewa continue, evolve, transition, transform?

For now, Wewa remains a place of sunshine and shadow, darkness and light, heat and humidity, beauty and danger, a place of crackers, loggers, farmers, and correctional guards, a small town of shotgun houses and a rural-route way of life, a region of longleaf pines, magnolia, and bald cypress trees, of raccoons, deer, rabbits, turtles, snakes, and alligators.

To call Wewa or the panhandle the Redneck Riviera or Alabama with a Florida zip code is too disrespectful, too dismissive, too simplistic for this extraordinary, complex, and utterly unique place.

For me this will always be the real Florida, not the manufactured or imported, not tacky or touristy, not Art Deco or amusement park, not invasive or intrusive like hydrilla in our waterways or pythons in the Everglades. But the great green northwest of millions of acres of bald-cypress swamps, dense hardwood hammocks, and longleaf and slash pine forests.

And as amazing as Wewa is, Reggie returning means it's about to get even better.

I try unsuccessfully to get someone to meet me at Tucks and so sit alone at one end of the bar nursing a bottle of hard lemonade.

It's a weeknight and more empty than not. Still, there's a couple shy of twenty people—a few guys shooting pool, a couple of couples shooting darts, a middle-aged man and not his wife on the dance floor, and a good-sized group at the opposite end of the bar from me.

Before me on the bar beside my phone is an order of buffalo shrimp and a small Styrofoam container of ranch—more to give me something to do than anything else. I had eaten earlier after seeing Reggie and am not hungry now, but the big Gulf shrimp bathed in Stacy's buffalo sauce and dipped in her ranch are irresistible.

I've been here a few hours. Not sure how much longer I'll stay. I really want to see Reggie but don't think I can take another Hank William Jr. song.

—You're a reporter, aren't you?

I turn to see a shortish, roundish youngish man with too many teeth and white puffy skin standing behind me, a blue bottle of Bud Light Platinum in his right hand.

—Used to be.

—What's-his-name McKnight.

—Merrick.

—That's right. I'm Dahl Rogers.

His words are slightly slurred and a decibel or two too loud.

The jukebox is between tunes and the other sounds in the bar are subdued. The chatter is mostly a hushed hum, only the occasional loud laugh or angry emphasized word.

Even in the absence of music the couple on the dance floor continues to slow dance, their movements more like dry humping than anything else.

Rogers bumps into my stool as he makes his way to the

one beside me and collapses onto it.

—You should do a story on that dirty rat bastard, he says.

He's wearing a baseball cap with a fishing store logo that can't hide the fact that he needs a haircut, wiry wisps of darkish locks curling up around the rim and beneath the brim.

—Which dirty rat bastard is that? I ask with a smile.

—There are a lot around here, I'll give you that. But I was talking about the biggest one of 'em all. Robin Wilson. Most crooked cop to ever wear the badge.

I had gone to school with Wilson. He had been a grade or two behind me. We had played ball together. And it has crossed my mind to write about him.

A large blonde girl feeds a couple of bucks into the jukebox and it comes to life again. Suddenly the space is filled with the soulful seventies-sounding sax as Bob Seger's *Turn the Page* starts to play.

—It's already being done.

FDLE is conducting an investigation into allegations of all manner of wrongdoing at this very moment and every newspaper in the area is covering it.

—Huh?

—Stories, I say. Lots of them being written about him.

—I ain't talkin' about that soft-serve shit they keep printing in the area cunt rags. I mean real news. Actual fuckin' reporting. Inside info. Names. Dates. Crimes. I got it all.

—Oh yeah? How's that?

—I used to work for his evil ass.

As we talk, a large, late-thirties, muscular man with a butch-waxed crew cut, who I recognize as one of Wilson's deputies, stares at Rogers menacingly from over near the pool table.

—How long ago?

—Huh?

—When'd you lose your job?

—Month or so back.

—How?

—He told me to lose the paperwork on an arrest I had

made. I told him to kiss my hairy white ass. Then he made up some bogus bullshit and fired me.

I nod.

Returning my attention to my drink, I take a final last long swallow and start to stand as Reggie walks in.

—You want the story or not? It ain't free. It's worth something and I got no income comin' in.

—Let's exchange numbers and talk tomorrow, I say, no intention of calling him.

I wave to Reggie and smile but before I can finish up with Rogers the group at the opposite end of the bar has rushed her and whisked her away.

—What's wrong, man? he asks.

—What?

—What's wrong? You look like you just—

—Nothing.

I scribble my number on a cocktail napkin, not wanting to enter his number into my phone. He does the same and we swap them.

—I'll try to call you tomorrow, I say.

As I'm placing the napkin with his number on it in my pocket, the crewcut, musclebound deputy is suddenly standing there beside us.

For a long, awkward moment he says nothing, just stands there staring, beer in one hand, pool stick in the other.

—Well, I'm gonna go, Rogers says.

—What's your hurry, Dahl? the deputy asks.

Rogers quickly and nervously drops his half-empty bottle on the bar and moves toward the door.

—Wait, the deputy says. How's the job hunt goin'?

Rogers keeps walking.

—I may have a line on somethin' for you, the deputy says.

Rogers bumps into the lone couple still slow dancing, apologizes, and continues.

—I'll walk you out, the deputy says, and turns to follow him.

I glance down the bar to see the small group at the other

end warmly welcoming Reggie back to town with back pats and bottles being passed around.

When I look back the deputy is at the door.

Dropping a twenty—the only cash I have—on the bar, I rush across the dance floor and out the door.

The mid-October night is clear and cold, the dirt parking lot dark and damp beneath a moonless sky.

The flashing lights on the arrow of the elevated reader board marquee sign reflect in a clay-colored mud puddle and off the vehicles close by.

There is no sign of Dahl Rogers or the deputy.

I scan the mud-splattered pickup trucks lined up in front between the building and the highway, then step off the small covered porch to the side lot and look through it. There are two cars and one jacked-up truck and no people.

Walking around to the back I find Dahl standing in the open doorway of his beat up old Chevrolet Impala, the deputy pressing in on him, pointing with his bottle of beer, his pool cue held down and out from his body a bit as if preparing to strike a blow.

—HEY, I yell.

The deputy turns and glares at me as I make my way across the lot to them, moist sand clinging to every step.

My heart is racing now and I am unsure of what I'm going to do.

—The fuck you want? the deputy asks.

—You said you had a job, I say.

—Yeah. So?

—Well . . . I need one. If Dahl's not interested I am.

—Huh?

—Is it a blow job or a hand job?

—The fuck d'you say?

—No, they get those from the inmates in the jail, Reggie says walking up behind me. Or is it y'all give them to the inmates?

—It's probably both, I say.

The deputy turns toward us, tossing his beer to the side and gripping his pool stick with both hands.

A Certain Retribution

As he does, Dahl gets in his car, closes and locks the door, cranks it and drives away.

—See how he grips his stick, Reggie says. There's our answer.

—He's a giver, I say.

—I'm gonna give you somethin' your faggot ass'll never forget, he says. That's for sure. Then I'm gonna—

He stops as he catches sight of Reggie as she comes up beside me.

His face lights up, eyes wide, inane smile.

—I remember you, he says with a sneer. I remember you real good. You're that little Sunset whore Allen used to dick. That's right . . . and not just Allen . . . This is gonna be fun. Who's first?

—Ladies first, Reggie says, stepping toward him with what looks like a small gun in her hand.

I stare at her in shock.

Zero to sixty. Just like that. The escalation is surreal. It was bad enough before, but now . . .

—Drop the stick, she says, pointing the gun at his overdeveloped pecks.

—Bitch, you just committed a felony, he says.

—Look at me, Donnie Ray, she says. You see anything in my eyes that makes you doubt I'll do it?

My mind is racing. Trying to come up with a way to defuse the situation. Think.

—You stupid bitch. I can't even see your eyes.

—Reggie, I say.

—Just a minute, Merrick.

—This is crazy, I say. Just—

Ignoring me, she continues to talk to Donnie Ray.

—I realize you're a bully with a badge most of the time, but right now you're just a drunk loser in a bar fight. And I wasn't the Sunset whore. I'm the Summers whore.

—Summers, he mutters.

—Last chance, she says. Drop the cue or I drop you.

He chuckles.

—Two words for you, she says. Bet you can't spell either

one. Neuromuscular incapacitation.

—Hell, I say, I'm a writer and I'd have a hard time with those.

Before I finish what I am saying, she fires the weapon—which turns out to be a Taser—the two dart-like electrodes penetrate his tight T-shirt and strike him in the chest, delivering an electrical current that disrupts Donnie Ray's voluntary muscle control and leads to the aforementioned neuromuscular incapacitation and the afore-promised drop.

Donnie Ray hits the damp ground hard, his pool stick landing on top of him.

—I thought you had a gun, I say. Thought you were about to shoot him.

—On our first date? she says. Not a chance. Don't want to scare you off.

—Peach, Reggie says when we're back inside, Donnie Ray is drunk as fuck again, passed out in the parking lot. Can you call someone to take him home?

—You got it, partner, Peach says. We're a full service joint.

We're standing near the middle of the bar. Peach is across from us, slinging bottles, popping caps. Behind us a couple of early twenties boys in tight jeans and even tighter T-shirts are taking their best shot at the punching bag. Old Crow Medicine Show is on the jukebox. Everyone is smiling and laughing and having a good time as the great wagon wheel of life keeps rolling along.

—If you were a full service lounge you'd have liquor, Reggie says, and a Platinum shuttle to get our asses home safely.

—First night back in town and already tryin' to change the joint. Let's at least drink about it. What'll y'all have?

—Bud Light, Reggie says. And . . .

—Mike's, I say.

—You got it.

A Certain Retribution

During our first drink we shoot the shit with Peach and eventually Stacy, after she closes the kitchen, and a few others happy to have Reggie back in town. After which we take our second drink to a table over by the wall for a little more intimate conversation.

—Scared you a little bit out back, didn't I? she says.
—Little bit, yeah.
—Have I scared you away yet?
I shake my head.
—Give me time. I will.
—You always armed? I ask.
—Always.

I nod and think about it. There's a story there. And it's probably about far more than being a woman in this wicked world, though that is justification enough from where I sit.

—What're you thinkin'? she asks.
—Just about that.
—I attract trouble, she says. And losers.
—Thanks, I say with a smile.
She laughs.
—You're not attracted to me.
—Actually I am.
—I'm not your type.
—I don't have a type but if I—
—Look at me, she says. I'm too big, too plain, too country for you.
—What you are is truly beautiful.
—To be honest you're not my type either.
I nod.
—Well then let's just enjoy our drinks and try not to tase anyone else.
—Donnie Ray and I have a history, she says. I know the sort of man he is. I'm pretty sure I saved you from an assault with a deadly pool cue.
—Probably did.
—You're welcome by the way.
I smile.
—I'm going to thank you, I say.

—I look forward to it.
—You moving back or just visiting? I ask.
—Moving.
—Why now? What brings you back home?
—Two reasons really. Maybe even three. At least one is a secret for another day or so, then everyone will know. The other is Rain is old enough to be able to see what a douche his dad is. But the main one is my mom is dying of cancer.
—Oh God, Reggie. I'm so sorry. I didn't know.
—We've never been close but . . . my sister's asshole husband won't let her move in with them . . . so . . . They've sent her home to die. Hospice has been called in. Rain and I will do what we can. Mostly just be with her.
—I'm really so, so sorry. I should've asked sooner.
—I'm fine. Not just sayin' it. I'm glad Rain gets this time with his grandma. I'm happy to help her, be here for her, but I'm not gonna let our entire existence be defined by her disease.
—Anything I can do, I say, any way I can help . . . with anything . . . just let me know.
She nods.
—I'm not just sayin' that. I really mean it.
—I know you do. Thank you.
—Where'd you move from? What did you do there and how'd you like it?
She smiles.
—Tampa. I've been a correctional officer, a prison investigator, and done some private security stuff. And since the moment I was stupid enough to get pregnant by Rain's douchey dad, how I like a thing—or whether or not I even do—is not relevant.
—Single motherhood, I say.
—Or somethin' like it.
George Strait's *You Look So Good in Love* comes on and one of the early twenties boys walks over and asks her to dance.
—That's sweet but I bet I went to school with your mama, Reggie says. And what would she say?
—More'n likely, Way to go, hero. Did you get some?
—It's what I'd say to my son. Your mom's alright. But

A Certain Retribution

I'm on a date, so the only one not gettin' some from me tonight will be him.

    She jerks her thumb toward me. The kid looks my way as if noticing me for the first time.

    —I'll be back, he says, glaring at me.

    —The answer will be the same, she says.

    He swaggers away.

    —Give my best to your mom, Reggie says.

Without turning back toward us, he slowly lifts his arm while continuing to walk, and gives us the finger.

    —I should probably go, she says. Big day tomorrow.

    —Can I follow you home?

    —In a non-stalkery way?

    I nod.

    —To walk you to your door. And to make sure you don't tase anyone else.

    —That's it?

    —You already told the kid I wasn't gettin' any.

    —You think Donnie Ray might try to retaliate? she says.

    —Thought had crossed my mind.

    —You don't think I can handle him?

    —In a fair fight, no question, but he doesn't strike me as the fair fighting type.

    —Neither am I.

    —Will you at least text me when you get there?

    —Damn it man, she says, don't give up so easily.

    —You still an investigative journalist? she asks.

    I laugh.

    —What?

    —Just sounds kinda grand for what I do.

    —That is what you do. The oil spill. The retirement homes. High school football concussion coverups. The water wars. The sex trafficking piece.

    —So you've read some of my work?

—I have, she says. Good shit. And there's only one name for it. Investigative journalism. So you still doing it or not?

I shrug.

We are sitting next to each other on the remnants of a rickety old dock behind her mom's elevated mobile home on the banks of the Apalachicola River, which as it turns out is only about half a mile from the small clapboard house I share with Casey and Kevin.

It's dark and most of what we can see is the outline of things, darker shapes on the darkness, but light from the landing and Gaskin Park and the camps and houses along Byrd Parker Drive provide enough illumination for us to see swaths of the river, random objects, and each other.

Across the way, on the opposite side of the river, an empty houseboat tied to the bank appears to have an apparition floating the length of its porch. An erie green glow. There, then gone.

—What does that mean? she asks. Isn't it sort of like being pregnant? You either are or you aren't.

—I'm doing a few special assignment pieces for an online startup that hasn't really—

—Hasn't really what?

—Started up.

—Oh.

—And I'm helping my dad a little with the *Breeze*, but I'm not on staff anywhere anymore.

She nods.

—I'm . . .

—What? she asks.

—I don't know, I say. Not even sure what I was going to say.

—And you're raising your step-kids?

I nod.

—Sort of. Casey's pretty much grown. Kevin's still a kid—always will be in a way I guess.

She looks puzzled.

—He has Autism.

—Wow. And you've got 'em by yourself?

A Certain Retribution

—They've lost both parents. I'm not much but I'm all they've got. When Monica died their bio dad took them away from me and made it very difficult for me to stay in touch. And I was pretty fucked up anyway. So I missed a few years with them. After their dad died and they moved back we reconnected, and they've been with me ever since.

—How the hell you making ends meet?

—Wouldn't say the ends are anywhere close to meeting. Why would you think they would be?

We fall quiet a moment.

My phone vibrates in my pocket and I pull it out in case it's Casey. I don't recognize the number and let it go to voicemail. Then see I've missed a text from Casey saying they're home safely and for me not to rush and to make sure to have a good time.

A brisk breeze ripples the surface of the water and blows up, rustling the tree branches and tousling our hair.

The greenish glow floats across the houseboat again.

—What's the story with the houseboat? I say.

—You have to swim over to find out.

—Don't want to know that bad. Hell, it was an idle curiosity.

—Damn it, man. Just say you're scared. No need for all the defensiveness. Tell you what. I've even got a little boat you can use. Paddle over instead of swim.

—I get anything if I do?

—Such as?

—I don't know, some sort of reward for bravery.

—Already told you . . . you ain't gettin' any . . . kinds of rewards tonight.

—Another time then, I say.

—Probably not.

—Why's that?

—Told ya. You're too . . . I'm not your type. Not looking for anything anyway.

—Methinks the lady doth protest too much.

—See? she says, as if I have just proven her point. Shit like that. Right there. You're too artsy for me, too nice. Hell, I think you might actually be a good guy. And I'm too country for you, too big, too plain. I drink Bud Light and watch NASCAR and like to shoot shit. I'm sure you're some sort of hippie environmentalist. I'm a conservative Republican. I bet you're a liberal Democrat.

She pauses and I don't say anything.

She feels so good sitting next to me, her body pressing against mine. Her hair smells of warm vanilla sugar, her breath of Trident Watermelon Twist, and I want to kiss her.

—Well? she says.

Before I can respond another breeze blows up off the dark waters and she shivers.

I take the opportunity to put my arm around her.

Holding her close to me, huddling together slightly more, I rub her arm.

—Wouldn't think someone as thick as me would get cold, but I am almost always cold.

I shake my head.

—Wouldn't think someone with such a great body would put it down, I say, but you almost always are.

She starts to say something, but before she can I lean in and kiss her.

It's a great first kiss. Her mouth is wet and warm and tastes of watermelon.

When I pull back she says *Thank you* in such a sweet, tender, genuine, and genuinely unexpected way, that I will never forget it for as long as I live.

Pleased with the response, I kiss her some more.

And it's as good as the first time. Maybe even better. And I can feel my body responding to hers.

When I pull back this time, I just sit there taking in her beauty, her warmth, her stunning eyes.

—What is it? she asks.

—Just thinking.

—What?

—Do all Republicans kiss as good as you?

A Certain Retribution

I am kissing her goodnight at her door a little later when her phone buzzes.

—Sorry, she says, pulling it out and looking at it. Shit.

She turns, opens the door, and rushes in, leaving it open. I hesitate at first then follow.

The old mobile home has been remolded. One great room that includes den, kitchen and dining room has windows running the length of the back wall overlooking the river.

Though old and poorly constructed, the place is immaculate, as clean as any home I've ever entered actually in use, the smell of Gain overriding that of anything else.

To the left a single hallway leads to the back part of the narrow single wide and the three bedrooms and one bath lining it.

Halfway down the hallway Reggie's mom, Sylvia, is on the floor, Rain, Reggie's son, trying to help her up.

—I'm okay. I'm okay. Don't make a fuss.

She is feeble and frail, her faded pink pajamas falling off her emaciated frame.

Seeing Sylvia splayed on the floor reminds me of the loss of my own mom like few things have in a long time, and a dull ache awakens at the center of me.

—Mom, you're not okay. You fell.

The worn linoleum floor and thin-paneled wall hallway is extremely narrow and I linger near the entrance, wanting to be close enough to help but far enough back to not intrude.

—I didn't fall. I really am okay. Promise.

—What happened?

—Walking back from the bathroom I just got weak and dizzy and started to . . .

—Fall, Reggie says.

—So I leaned against the wall and just kind of slowly slid down. I didn't fall. Then I just sat here and got my bearings. I'm okay now. I so didn't want to disturb you, interrupt your date, so I called Rain out to help me up and he insisted he had to call you. I'm fine now. Really.

—You sure?

—Positive. Just need help getting back to bed.

—Mom, Rain, this is Merrick, Reggie says, nodding back toward me.

—'Sup? Rain says.

He's a small-framed, muscular boy in only athletic shorts, with long, straight brown hair, and burn scars on his back.

—I remember Merrick, Sylvia says. I read all your articles in the paper. Love the way you write.

—Thank you. Can I help?

—That's kind of you but I'd die of embarrassment. Reggie can help me. She's strong as an ox. All us Summers women are. Least I used to be.

—Rain, Reggie says, back to bed. Merrick, back outside.

—Night, love you, Rain says.

—Night. Love you. And thank you. You did the right thing. Don't listen to your grandma. Always call me.

Rain disappears into his room and closes the thin door.

—It was good to see you, Merrick, Sylvia says. Even under the circumstances. Come back for a proper dinner sometime soon.

—Thank you. I will. Was good to see you too.

As, I ease back down the hallway and into the great room, my phone vibrates in my pocket again. I withdraw it to see that I'm getting another call from another number I don't recognize.

Stepping out onto the front stoop and closing the door behind me, I take the call.

—Hello.

—This is Sergeant Thompson with the Gulf County Sheriff's Department. Who 'm I speaking to?

I don't recognize the name or the voice but would be surprised if I don't know him—or at least of him. Wewa is a small town. Gulf is a small county. Of course he could be from Port St. Joe, the town on the other end of the county, in which case chances are still good I'd know him. Just not as good.

After decades of having a police force of one, the City of Wewahitchka decided to disband its police department,

A Certain Retribution

contracting instead with the Gulf County Sheriff's Department to provide deputies to patrol. Since many of the deputies are from the other end of the county, they're often not familiar to me.

—Merrick McKnight.

—Hey Merrick, he says in a way that lets me know he knows me. Where're you?

—Not far from my house, I say. What is it? What's wrong?

—Sheriff wants to talk to you. Hold on a sec.

I wait as the phone is passed, wondering what's going on, grateful to have heard from Casey and to know she and Kevin are safe at home.

—Merrick? Robin Wilson says.

—Yeah?

—Hey Merrick, it's Robin. Hey man, I need your help with something.

Even though we went to school together and were at one time sort of friends it surprises me he says Robin instead of Sheriff Wilson.

He is smooth and politiciany and buddy-buddy in a certain Southern boy trying to be charming way. He oozes friendship and good ol' boy mannerliness and has himself convinced he's not bent. Which is what makes it so easy for him to convince others.

—Okay?

—Did you talk to Dahl Rogers tonight?

—Yeah.

—What time?

—Not sure. We were at Tucks. I can probably figure it out to be more exact if you need me to but I'd guess around eight.

—Not since then?

—No. Why?

—Merrick, Dahl was killed tonight, and your number was the last one he called.

After explaining to Reggie why and where I'm going, I'm driving along the twisting and turning Lake Grove Road away from the river toward the crime scene.

Thoughts of Reggie and our night together compete with those of Dahl Rogers and Donnie Ray and my interactions with them.

Reggie is right. We are extremely different. And both dealing with so much right now. Between Kevin's condition and her mom's, there's no time for much of anything at the moment. And that would presuppose we even want something, which I'm not sure I do and she seems fairly certain she doesn't.

Still, there's something there. I know she feels it too. Why else would she have spent most of the night with me? Especially given what she's dealing with at home. Maybe that's the only reason she did it. Could be.

But that kiss, man. I mean damn. And the easy way we were together.

She's clearly wounded. So defensive. Hell, offensive too. She's always armed. And trigger happy as hell with her Taser.

She has armor sure, but you can tell there's real tenderness beneath it. My guess is her heart is so big and beautiful she had to construct the armor just to survive.

Even if that's true, you've sworn off women for a while. You said after Regan you were done for—

It's been a while.

True, but you could stand to wait a little longer. Plus you said no more wounded women.

We're all wounded.

You know what I mean.

She's so strong. So tough. Single mom. Taking care of her kid all these years on her own. And now her mom.

But her heart is damaged. She told you herself. She's attracted to losers, to emotionally unavailable bad boys.

You're right. She's not interested in me. All of this is moot anyway.

What just happened? she wonders.
Something unexpected as hell, that's what.
I actually don't want to see him go. What the hell?
Is he as interested as he seems? Is that possible?
It was just tonight. He got caught up. That's all. Besides, no way any man is that nice, that kind and attentive.
Seemed genuine. Certainly what I remember of him from school was like that.
If it is then he's not interested in you.
But the way he kissed me. That damn kiss was something else now. Wow.
Cher's version of *It's in His Kiss* begins to play in her head.
Does he love me? I wanna know . . .
Stop it.
She tries to, but as she does *Kiss on My List* takes its place. *My friends wonder why I call all you the time. What can I say?*
He won't be calling again and you know it. You're being silly and childish. Quit acting so high school.

In a wooded area on a two-trail dirt road inside the empty Seven Springs Lake subdivision, less than half a mile from where I had last seen him in the Tukedawayz parking lot, Dahl's dead body sits slumped in his still, idling Chevrolet Impala.
One of many vacant subdivisions in the area, Seven Springs Lake off the lower Land's Landing Road has paved streets, dotted with ornate street lamps, winding around empty foreclosed lots now owned by the banks. Planned, developed, and partially sold during the recent real estate boom, it sits languishing and unfinished since the more recent real estate bust. The few lots in it that were actually sold were purchased

for investment purposes by people who had every intention of flipping them for a profit. Caught without a soft place to land in the high stakes game of real estate musical chairs, those who couldn't afford to hold on to property they had pledged to pay ten times what it was suddenly worth quit making payments, leaving banks and ultimately taxpayers as the real last ones standing and therefore losers of the game. A game the taxpayers didn't even know they were playing.

Turning right off Land Drive into Seven Springs I see the flashing lights of patrol cars, an ambulance, and the sheriff's department crime scene van blocking the road about a quarter mile down.

The entrance to Seven Springs is marked by an elaborate Asian-influenced structure meant to hold the now missing sign. Something about its design reminds me of Grauman's Chinese Theatre in Hollywood.

I pull up and park several car lengths behind the nearest cruiser and get out.

Robin is waiting for me.

—Sheriff, I say.

—Hey Merrick, he says, and it's amazing how much is conveyed in the way he says it—familiarity, friendship, faux sincerity, gratitude, camaraderie, sadness.

He leads me down the asphalt road between the vehicles.

The uninhabited neighborhood is eerie in the dark night, particularly with the splash of emergency light flashing on the limbs, leaves, and shafts of trees.

The silence adds to the uncanniness, the wind and the hushed hum of the idling cars the only sounds.

We enter the overgrown two-trail dirt lane, a canopy of weight-bent branches above us, the cold, hard, damp earth beneath our feet, and I wonder again why he's asked me here, why he insists on showing me. Does he really think I had something to do with Dahl's death? Or does he think I'm investigating him and wants to know what Dahl has told me?

The narrow to begin with path is made more so by the understory growth toward the middle, tiny branches and bushes reaching for one another across the small divide. Nature abhors a vacuum.

As we go deeper and deeper in, as even the flashing light from the vehicles on the paved road fades, it grows even darker and more disquieting, and I wonder if Robin is bringing me back here to set me up or kill me.

The sweet smells of hay, horses, and manure drift over from an unseen but nearby pasture. It make me think of Reggie, who in high school was a serious horse riding cowgirl, often competing in horse shows and rodeos. I smile in the dark as I think of her and the night we just had, and wish I could be somewhere warm with her right now.

We arrive at a small intersection of sorts where another two-trail dirt roadway crosses the one we're on.

The area is littered with beer bottles, large plastic Subway cups, aluminum soft drink and Red Bull cans, 5-hour Energy drink bottles, assorted pieces of paper and bags, the charred remnants of small campfires, and a pile of blue, red, and purple Swisher Sweets mini cigarillo pouches so thick it looks like a stack of tickets.

—Just a little farther, he says.

We walk another twenty feet or so to just around a soft bend in the road to find a middle-aged deputy standing next to Dahl's idling Impala.

Backlit by the car's taillights, the deputy is a black mass outlined by a raw red glow, appearing like an angry apparition, exhaust from the car adding to the illusion.

Robin and the deputy exchange greetings.

—Now Merrick, Robin says as he turns to me, it's bad, so you need to prepare yourself. Okay?

I nod.

—Looks like he shot himself in the head and . . . well . . . the entire car is a mess of brains and blood.

I nod again.

—You sure you're up for this?

—Yeah, I say, but why do you even want me to look? What can I possibly—

—Look around, he says. Nobody out here but you, me, and Deputy Robertson. I haven't even let crime scene out here yet. No one else has been out here but us and the kids who found him.

—Who did find him?

—You remember Melody Ann? Went to school with us. Her daughter Katie and her boyfriend—Ben Little's boy, Taylor. Shook 'em up bad. I think they come out here to make love and saw the taillights. They said they were headed to the gazebo 'cause Taylor left his phone earlier today when Anitra Mayhann brought 'em out here to take pictures of 'em.

The developers had built a gazebo next to the lake for residents of the Seven Springs Lake neighborhood to use. Since there have been no residents over the years, the gazebo, a large well-built structure in the woods, has been used by teens as a place to hang out and make out and as a popular spot for portraits and prom pictures to be taken.

I look around, trying to figure out where the gazebo is in relation to the car.

—You don't have any idea why Dahl called you tonight? Robin asks.

I shake my head.

—You didn't answer and he didn't leave a message?

—Right. I didn't recognize the number and I didn't pick up.

—And he didn't leave you a message?

—No.

—No one else has been out here but us, he says. No one has touched anything. We haven't let crime scene in to process anything.

I think about that.

—Somebody checked his phone, I say.

He nods.

—You're right, he says. I did that. It was calling that number and having you answer it that gave me the idea.

—What idea?

—I'm sure you know about the allegations against me and that my department is being investigated by FDLE.

I nod.

—Have you written anything about it? I haven't seen

anything.

    I shake my head.

    He nods.

    —I appreciate that. Well, anyway, the thing is, Merrick, I'm under a lot of scrutiny right now. I haven't done anything wrong. I swear it. But you know how these things work. People believe what they read. They just do. Thing is, Dahl was one of my men. A brother in arms. I had to let him go and it broke my heart, but he was wrong and it had to be done. The thing is, I'm pretty sure he's been going around telling anyone who would listen that I'm dirty and he had proof. I don't know if FDLE had interviewed him yet or not but it was just a matter of time. Anyway, people're gonna think his death is some sort of cover-up, that me or my men did this. And I can't get a fair shake from any of the other news outlets in the area. All they want is a good story that sells papers, so they want my department to be corrupt. But it's not. At least not to my knowledge. So here's what I was thinking, Merrick, and you tell me what you think about it. You follow the investigation from the very beginning all the way through. You do your investigative journalism thing with full access, and tell the truth all along the way. I think it could be very good for you. I know things haven't been easy for you lately. And it'd help me. The truth is on my side and I just want it out there. Whatta you say?

    Merrick gone, her mom and Rain in bed, Reggie pulls out her files from their secret secure location in the locked metal file box and pours over them as she had so many times before.

    But it's different this time.

    Before, the men in the files were figments of memory and imagination, mythic creatures born of brutality and fed by trauma, but now she had come face to face with one, stared down the demon and won round one.

    But he's not a demon. Just a man. A blunt, benighted bully, capable of cruelty and savagery, but no more. Nothing mythic. Nothing supernatural. Nothing she couldn't put down like a deranged dog.

She looks again at the pictures of Donnie Ray she had printed from the Internet and inserted in his file when she began formulating her foray into restorative justice so long ago, comparing him with the brutish boy she remembered and the rapacious man she encountered earlier in the night.

Just a man, she thinks. Just a mad dog of a man in need of putting down.

She has a decision to make.

Does she get involved now? Take over the investigation tonight?

She has little doubt that Robin Wilson is behind what has happened to Dahl Rogers—whether directly or through Donnie Ray or another of his deputies—and if she waits she runs the risk of his contaminating the crime scene and the investigation beyond recovery. But if she doesn't wait she could jeopardize the other, larger investigation.

Could she even step in tonight if she wanted to? She officially starts tomorrow after the city commissioners' meeting, which means she has no authority until then.

Damn it!

She's not good at waiting. Can't stand to not be doing something.

Doing something too soon is the best way to fuck it up. She knows that from experience.

You've waited this long to make them pay. Don't be stupid. It's gonna take even more patience to bring down the crooked fucker.

The truth is she hasn't been waiting patiently. Waiting at all had not been something she'd done willingly. She had been forced to wait. And that had been hard has hell. Now that she is actually this close, now that she actually has an opening, and opportunity, it's going to be impossible to wait.

And yet you have to.

Maybe not.

Instead of just sitting here maybe there's something she can do tonight, right now, this minute.

A Certain Retribution

She smiles as she reaches for her phone.

Doing something beats hell out of not. It sure as shit does.

The time on her phone reads two-twenty. So much for a good night's sleep before her big day.

She knows Peach will be up. Hell, she may still be at the bar. What she doesn't know is if she still has the same number.

But after two rings, she picks up.

—You okay? Peach asks by way of answering.

—Yeah.

—Let me guess. You and ol' Merrick are bogged down in Iola and need me to come pull you out.

—Good guess but that's not it tonight.

—Then how can I help you?

—Who'd you call to pick up Donnie Ray?

—Hoss.

—Ross the Hoss Redmon?

—The one and only.

—When'd he come and get him?

—Wasn't more'n about ten minutes after I called him I'd say.

—What'd he do? Did he stay?

—Gathered him up and took off. TicTac had to help get 'im in the truck.

—He couldn't get in the truck by himself?

—Bastard couldn't get off the ground by himself.

—Can I get Ross's number from you?

—Damn, Reggie. Two in one night.

—That ain't funny, Peach.

—I'll give you his number, but hell, he's right here. I could just give him the phone.

—No. Don't do that. Just make sure he doesn't leave before I get there. I'm on my way.

—Shit, he ain't goin' anywhere anytime soon. Andrea Ake's got him bayed up like a big bloated boar hog.

—On my way.

—If you really want to remove all suspicion you should let FDLE process the scene and conduct the investigation, I say.

—Merrick, I know what you mean, Robin says, I do, but I can't. I wish I could. I really do. But I just can't. They're the ones investigating me and I'm gonna tell you, at least one of the investigators has already made up his mind.

I think about it.

—If I do it, I'm going to do it all the way. Full access. Nothing held back from me. And I'm going to tell the truth whatever it is.

—That's why I'm asking you. I don't read much news. Know enough to know most of it is bullshit. But I read that piece you did on sex trafficking. It was amazing. Fair. Honest. You've got integrity.

I think about how many threats I still get from that piece.

—What about another department? I say. Why not ask the Bay County Sheriff's Department to conduct the investigation? You know McKeithen will be honest and fair.

—Merrick, I'm gonna conduct this investigation. I'm gonna find out if Dahl killed himself or if someone else did. If it's someone else, I'm gonna find them and lock them up. And I'm gonna do all this by the book. I have to. My department is under more scrutiny than you can imagine. Now, I'm givin' you a chance to observe and write about it and make sure I do my job with integrity and report to the people of our county what the truth is. It's up to you. But you've got to decide now. I've got to get started.

When Reggie arrives at Tucks less than ten minutes later, the place is clearing out and Peach is locking up.

—You closin'?

—Yeah. Didn't realize how late it was.

A Certain Retribution

—Where's Ol' Hoss?

Before she can answer Ross Ol' Hoss Redmon stumbles out of the bathroom.

—Reggie Summers? Is that you? Goddamn girl. As I live and breathe. Haven't seen you in a couple of coons ages. How the hell are you, darlin'?

He's a tall, emaciated man with weathered skin, a Fu Manchu mustache, and long salt-and-pepper hair worn in a perpetual ponytail. As if a uniform, all these years later he's still wearing faded blue jeans, cowboy boots, a wife beater no matter the temperature, and his signature enormous silver-and-gold belt buckle depicting a rodeo rider on a bucking bronco. Because he's so short-waisted, his long legs seem to go on forever and his belt buckle appears to be just beneath his chest.

—Good Ol' Hoss. How about you?

—You look good, gal. You growed up all good and shit. You still ridin'?

—Not much these days. Little here and there when I can. Don't have my own horse anymore. You?

—Often as these old bones'll let me.

—I miss it.

—I got horses need ridin'. Hell, can't get to them all. Any time you wanna ride just saddle up.

—Thanks man. 'Preciate that.

—Anything for you, cowgirl.

—Anything?

—Hell yeah. Whatcha got on your mind?

—Need your help.

—Hell, name it.

—You picked up Donnie Ray earlier tonight?

—Yeah, I picked up that sorry piece of shit. 'Scuse my French, missy. But he is. I mean by god but he's a big giant dick ache.

—What'd you do with him?

—Took him home.

—How was he?

—Hell, I had to carry him in. Just dropped his sorry ass on the couch and left him there. Last time too. Tappin' out on taking care of all these drunk ass dandies 'round here. Hell, just 'cause we went to school together don't mean I got to play fuckin' nurse maid the rest of my goddamn life. 'Scuse my French two times.

—How far he live from here?
—Not far.
—You take me to his house?
—Hell yeah. Why?
—Just need to ask him somethin'.
—Truck's out front. Let's go. Only, can Andrea Ake come too? Told her I'd give her a ride.
—I bet you did.
—Come on, man. It ain't exactly like that.
—If it ain't I bet it's pretty damn close. Tell you what. We'll be quick. Let her stay here with Peach. Tell her you'll be back in no time to give her all the ride she can handle.
—Ten-four.
—And I'll drive, Reggie says. You grab shotgun and navigate.
—Hell, ain't much to navigate. He just lives a little ways down Land's Landing Road.

Which means, Reggie thinks, it's less than a mile from the crime scene.

Dahl's white 2005 Chevrolet Impala and the area around it is now lit by banks of generator-powered halogen lights and swarmed by investigators and crime scene technicians.

The vehicle, a former cop car Dahl bought at auction, is filthy and still bears much of the decal glue from its former life.

—Crazy son of a bitch, Robin says. Driving an old cop car. It's like he never wanted to feel off duty.

We are standing back about ten feet, watching the crime scene being processed.

The area around the car is being scoured for evidence, as is the exterior of the car.

A Certain Retribution

Pictures are taken, casts and measurements made, potential evidence bagged and tagged.

From the other side of the car comes laughter.

—HEY, Robin yells. None of that. This is one of our own. It's Dahl y'all. Come on. Accord him the respect he deserves.

Transitioning to the interior of the car, the lead investigator, Perry Griffin, opens the driver's side door with a gloved hand.

Across from him a female crime scene tech attempts the same but finds it locked.

—Check the other ones, Griffin says.

The two back doors are found to be locked also.

—So, Griffin says in the general vicinity of the female deputy taking notes and the male tech videoing, only the driver's side door is unlocked.

Without touching anything, Griffin leans in and looks at the body and around the interior of the car.

—The deceased has an apparent gunshot wound to the right back side of the head, Griffin says. There's a revolver on the passenger side floorboard.

He then steps back and lets the photographer and videographer go to work.

After they've gotten everything they can from the one open door, the others are opened and they shoot everything from those angles as well.

When that is complete, the ME goes to work on the body, taking temperatures and measurements and making the initial examination, as crime scene techs dust the vehicle for prints.

—So why do you think Dahl called you tonight? Robin asks.

—I'm not sure. At Tucks he told me he wanted to talk to me. We exchanged numbers. We were supposed to talk tomorrow.

—About?

I shrug, not sure how much to say.

I don't trust Robin but I also have no intention of

withholding vital information from the investigation.

—He said something about losing his job. Wanted to tell me his story.

—He thinks I fi—thought I fired him unjustly. To what . . . cover up some of my crimes?

—You tell me.

—I had no choice but to fire him, Merrick. I didn't want to. Especially with the investigation going on. I gave him a thousand chances. He didn't take any. You're welcome to look over my notes and his file.

I nod.

—So what happened that made him call you tonight? he asks.

—He could've just butt dialed me, I say. Maybe he was entering my number and hit it. Maybe he thought of something else or decided it couldn't wait until tomorrow. Maybe he was drunk. Or maybe it could have something to do with his death. He saw something or someone. If he thought he was in danger maybe he called for help—though I don't think he'd call me for that unless he just panicked and my number was the one he hit. Or if he was really thinking about killing himself, maybe he wanted to talk to someone. Maybe I could've talked him out of it. I wish I had answered.

—Now Merrick, don't go beatin' yourself up over—

—I'm not, I say, an edge to my voice showing my frustration at his attempts at manipulation.

—Good, he says. There's no way you could have known.

—There's one other possibility, I say.

—Oh yeah? What's that?

—He and Donnie Ray were having words in the parking lot at Tucks. Seemed to be escalating. I stepped in and Dahl sped away. Maybe he felt bad about it. Or wanted to see if I was okay.

—Donnie Ray Kemp? My deputy?

I nod.

—He came after me with a pool stick after I interrupted him and Dahl.

Robin shakes his head.

A Certain Retribution

—Damn it, Donnie Ray. I'm sorry Merrick. When he gets to drinkin'. . . I'm not gonna have my men actin' like that. I'll put him on suspension tomorrow.

—Given the way he was acting, I'd say he's got to top your suspect list for this. If it turns out Dahl was murdered.

She finds Donnie Ray on the wide, well-worn couch inside the small cinderblock house he inherited from his grandmother. He appears to still be incapacitated, though she knows there's no way he could be from the Taser.

He is lying facedown on the couch, fully clothed. His body is at an odd angle, face pressed up into the corner, one leg partially hanging off, the toe of his boot touching the floor.

—Just how I dropped him, Hoss says. He ain't moved an inch.

—Donnie Ray, she says.

He doesn't respond.

—Donnie Ray, she says louder.

Still nothing.

—Hey Donnie Ray, Ol' Hoss is here to suck your dick. Roll over so he has some hope of finding the little fella.

—What the hell, man? Hoss says.

—Roll him over for me.

—For what?

—Not to suck his dick.

—Why are we here? What's this about?

—Roll him over. I need to see something.

He does as he's told, grabbing Donnie Ray by the arm and pulling him over, then taking a step back.

The momentum causes Donnie Ray to slide off the end of the couch and fall to the floor, his head thudding loudly on the hard tile.

He still doesn't rouse.

—Damn, Hoss says. Is he dead?

—Dead men don't breathe, Ol' Hoss. It's like a thing.

—Well why ain't he movin'?
—Was he like this when you brought him here?
—What? Passed out? Yeah.
—Didn't move? Didn't say a word?
—Right. Exactly like this.

She squats down beside Donnie Ray and slaps him hard on the face. Then again. And again.

The only reaction is an unpleasant expression and an unintelligible mumble.

—The hell're you doin'? Hoss asks.
—Got to make sure he's not faking.
—Faking what?
—Being passed out.

She pulls out a small vintage stag handle Ka-Bar pocket knife from her jeans, opens it, and begins to poke at Donnie Ray with it.

—Hell man, he's not faking, Hoss says. No way he could—

He stops when she begins to poke pretty hard at Donnie Ray's crotch.

—Shit Reggie. Come one. No way a man could not react to that. Satisfied now?
—Only way I could be completely satisfied would be to cut it off.

He starts to say something then stops, and she can tell he's remembering the prom all those years ago. It's obvious, unlike her, he doesn't think about it every day.

—Did he . . . Was he . . .
—Come on, she says. Let's go.

She stands, closing her grandfather's knife and returning it to her pocket, and begins moving toward the door without waiting for him.

—Wait, he says. What does it matter? Why would he fake being passed out?
—To make us think he didn't kill Dahl Rogers.
—Dahl Rogers is dead?
—Remember those flashing lights in Seven Springs?
—That was for Dahl? Hell cuz, Dahl, I mean goddamn.

And Donnie Ray did it?

—Not unless he's got no feeling in his nuts at all, she says.

It takes a while for Dahl's car to be processed. Whether because Dahl had been a fellow officer or because their department is being investigated or for my benefit, I find myself impressed by how careful, professional, and thorough the entire procedure is.

As I'm taking notes on my phone, I am surprised to get a couple of calls and texts from Reggie.

you okay? she texts when I don't answer her call.

Yes. Still at scene.

really? you sure youre okay need me to come over there

Her texts are short on capitalization and punctuation and are a challenge to follow at a glance.

I'm fine.

will you call me when they let you go

It'll be late.

please need to talk to you

Sure.

Eventually, the area, the car, and the body are processed and complete, and Griffin and the ME join me and Robin.

—Looks like suicide to me, Griffin says. We got no prints outside the vehicle, no evidence of any kind anyone else was out here. All the doors but his were locked. He was shot on the right side, so if someone else did it they'd have to be in the passenger seat or in the back and there's just nothing to suggest anyone was.

Robin nods and looks at the middle-aged ME.

—Doc?

The ME is from Bay County. Gulf County doesn't have one. He is a weary-looking man with wiry gray hair, wide hips, and thick glasses he touches a lot.

—I don't want to say much until after the autopsy, and

there are a few things that bother me, but at the moment I don't have any direct evidence to contradict the conclusions Detective Griffin is reaching.

Robin shakes his head then looks at me.

—Do you know that last year nearly as many cops killed themselves as died in the line of duty?

I shake my head.

—We got something like a suicide every sixteen minutes in this country and too many of 'em are cops. Dahl had his issues but he wasn't a bad cop. I feel like I failed him.

—Don't know what else you could've done for him, Sheriff, Griffin says. No one would've been as patient with him as you were.

—Should've seen the signs. Should've gotten him some help.

—That's on all of us, but I never saw any signs of something like this. Not sure there were any to see.

—There were. I just didn't see them.

—You said a few things bother you, I say to the ME. Like what?

He looks at Robin.

—This is Merrick McKnight.

—I know who he is. He's interviewed me before.

—You can say anything in front of him and please answer any questions he has. I've asked him to serve as watchdog over this investigation.

He nods.

—I'm not willing to say anything definitively until I've completed the autopsy and gotten back all the test results, but . . . well, the gun was farther away from the body than I would've expected. It was in the far upper corner of the passenger side floorboard. I'm not saying it couldn't have fallen that far, but I find it surprising that it did. That's all.

—What else? I ask.

—Where he was shot. Most self-inflicted gunshot wounds to the head are in the front or on the side. The back usually indicates someone else did the shooting. This one is on the right side of the head but far back enough to make me

question it. Seems an awkward angle.
　—Anything else?
　—There are two rounds missing from the revolver. We can only account for one shot being fired in the car. There's no note. Only about one in six leave one so I'm not saying it means anything. In fact, all of my questions are just that—questions. Issues and inconsistencies I have to explore, which I will thoroughly.
　—Is there anything else? I ask.
　—Only one other worth mentioning. He's wearing a ball cap. Shot went right through it.
　—Yeah? Robin says. What does that—
　—Typically people who commit suicide with a firearm don't shoot through clothing. They remove it or pull it back to expose skin. Usually, if a round has been fired through an article of clothing it means it's more likely a homicide than suicide.

　—Good God, son, are you and Robin Wilson engaged? Reggie says when she answers the phone.
　She answers on the first ring and doesn't sound sleepy.
　—We're definitely in bed together, I say.
　—Come again.
　—Well, at least embedded.
　—Does he really suspect you?
　—I don't think so.
　—Trying to pin it on you?
　—You never know with someone like him, but I don't think so.
　—Why have you come to the crime scene at all? Why keep you so long? What the hell is going on?
　—He asked me to follow the investigation from beginning to end and report on it.
　—Come again now?
　I did, telling her what he said and what we did.
　—The hell is he up to?
　—I've tried and tried to figure it out and can't really

come up with anything.
 —This is about to get real interesting.
 —Thought it already had, I say.
 —I meant for you and me.
 —How's that?
 —You're in a very unique position to help me, she says.
 —With your obvious sexual frustration?
 She laughs.
 It's an amused laugh, a surprised but in a good way laugh, a laugh that says the door is ajar to at least the possibility of that eventuality. It's a great laugh.
 —You stood there and watched them do everything tonight? she asks.
 —And asked questions and took notes, I say.
 —Oh wow. You are a godsend, aren't you?
 —Yes I am, I say. You wanna tell me how?
 —Starting tomorrow that'll be my investigation, she says. And I'll need everything you got on it tonight.
 —Wait. What? How will it be your—
 —I'm offering you a scoop here, Mr. Reporter Man. You want it or not? An honest to God story to break before anyone else does.
 —I'm about to pass your place, I say. Can we finish this conversation in person?

 When she opens the door, I step forward and kiss her. She kisses back.
 She is wearing long, loose flannel pajama bottoms and a University of Florida sweatshirt with no bra underneath. Her feet are covered in thick gray socks. She doesn't match for shit and she couldn't be sexier.
 —We already to that point in our relationship where you don't care about your appearance anymore? I ask.
 —You stop by in the wee hours of the morning, you get what you get.

A Certain Retribution

—Actually, you look cute and snuggly as fuck, I say, and hug and kiss her some more.

—Come in, she says, it's cold.

I do.

The trailer is dim and quiet and we pad silently over to the couch.

—Be honest, she says. Did you come by to finish the conversation in person or make out?

—Yes.

I lean in and kiss her some more, hugging and caressing her as I do. With one hand on her cheek, the other roams her body. But when I cup her breast through her sweatshirt she moves my hand.

—Really? I ask.

She laughs.

We go back to kissing and my hand goes right back to her breast. And again she moves it.

—Really? I say. I mean, really?

—Really.

—Not even on top of the clothes stuff?

—Not even upstairs outsidesies.

I laugh.

—Okay, I say with a sigh.

—Hey sailor, I appreciate the attempt. I really do. Don't give up.

I move my hand toward her breast again and she catches it and laughs.

—I didn't mean now, she says.

—Oh.

—Try again on our fourth date—if there is one. And if there's not then there was no reason to rev up the ol' engine anyway, now was there?

—So our next date, I say.

—Where'd you go to school, Wewa high? Our next date will be—

—Four, I say. Tonight at Tucks was our first. On the dock here was our second. And this is our third.

—Slow your roll there, partner. Anything that happened

tonight is all part of the same first date. And hell, I ain't even sure it counts at all. I met you at Tucks. You didn't take me. I drove myself home. You didn't. So actually we haven't even had our first date yet.

—So . . . Reggie . . . I was wondering . . . what are you doing tomorrow night? Would you like to go out with me?

—I can't tomorrow night, remember? That's the real reason you're here. Tomorrow's the big day.

—The day you take over the investigation into Dahl's death?

—Actually, I started tonight. I've ruled out Donnie Ray. He was still passed out when we went to his house.

—You went to his house tonight?

—Uh huh.

—Who's we?

—Ross the Hoss was with me. He's the one who gave Donnie Ray a ride home.

I don't say anything. Just think about it.

—You jealous? she asks.

—Little bit, yeah, I say with a smile.

—Don't be. Hell, Ol' Hoss had a date waitin' on him. I ain't stupid enough to get involved with anyone right now, but if I was it'd be you.

—That's so sweet, I say. You're the first girl to say she would get involved with me if she were just a little more stupid.

—It'd be more than a little more.

—Well, anyway, it's so sweet and means so much.

We are quiet a long moment, each still touching the other.

From the bedroom at the end of the hall the sounds of her mother's labored breathing can be heard. The night is so dark the windows along the back are opaque, showing only a dim reflection of the two of us huddled on the couch.

—Tomorrow's not just the day I take over the investigation into Dahl's death, she says. It's also the beginning of the end for Robin Wilson.

—How so?

—Just come to the city commissioners' meeting

tomorrow and you'll find out. And bring pen and paper, newspaper boy.

—Wewa City Commissioners' meeting?

She nods.

—Why? What happens there?

—The commissioners are voting to revoke the contract for Wilson's crooked ass to provide services to the city and are reinstating their own police department.

—Really? Wow.

—Uh huh.

—That is big. Man. Do they know something? Does FDLE have a case against Robin? Is he about to be arrested?

—Don't think they know anything the public doesn't know yet. They know he's corrupt and it's only a matter of time until he goes down, and they just don't want to be associated with his evil ass anymore. But all they have to say is they're not satisfied with the service the city is receiving any longer.

—Do they have someone lined up to be chief of police? I ask. Who's gonna have the job that will forever be thought of as belonging only to Preacher Glass?

—You're looking at her in her mismatched pajamas, she says. You've been trying to cop a feel from the new chief of police of the great town of Wewahitchka, Florida.

The next morning I meet Dad at the Corner Café for breakfast.

All around the restaurant, like the town, everyone is abuzz with news about last night. It's all anyone can talk about.

Word spreads fast in a small town.

—Did you hear there was a murder-suicide last night, someone standing at the counter is saying to Mitchell Johnson, the owner. A cop killed his wife then turned the gun on himself.

Fast, but rarely accurately.

—I don't think that's exactly what happened, Mitchell is saying, his patient manner polite and pleasant.

Michael Lister

Mitchell Johnson is a kind, early fifties African-American man who grew up here, moved away, then, like Reggie and me, moved back. He operates the Corner Café in a building on Main Street that was a drugstore when I was a kid and an Apostolic storefront church when I moved back. He owns it and the small building next to it that was a whites-only game room he was kept out of as a kid.

Michael Lister walks in and over to the doughnut counter, greeting Mitchell as he does.

—You read his new book yet? Dad asks.

—Not yet. I got it. Just haven't started it.

—It's good.

—I want his job, I said.

—I didn't know you wanted to write novels.

—Sometimes. Hell, I don't know what I want.

Our attention was drawn back to the counter.

—I heard it was a civilian killed by a cop, a recently retired teacher known for gossiping said.

Michael and Mitchell glance at the lady and shake their heads.

—You know Robin Wilson is under investigation, a short, fat middle-aged man in an ill-fitting jogging suit says. Probably had something to do with it. Ain't sayin' he done everthin' they're sayin', but he's done plenty. Gua-ran-tee that. Anywhere they's that much smoke they's bound to be fire.

Mitchell had started serving doughnuts again and people were coming and going as they had when he first opened as a doughnut shop under the name Basic Sweets, the electronic door ding sounding every few seconds.

—You believe this? Dad says.

—The death or the ridiculous rumors?

—Both.

I nod.

I'm having a sausage biscuit and coffee. Dad's working on a couple of doughnuts and a plastic bottle of skim milk.

—It's all anyone can talk about. Go in Harold's, K-Leigh's, the Express Lane, Dixie Dandy, IGA, you'll hear this same conversation going on.

A Certain Retribution

—Imagine so, I say.

—It's big news. Biggest this little town's seen in a while.

He smells a story and the promise of newspaper sales, maybe even the hint of a resurrection of sorts for the battered old *Breeze*.

Though there was a newspaper called the *Wewa News* that dates back to the 1800s when Wewahitchka was still part of Calhoun County, the *Breeze* was started in 1925, when C.F. Hanlon came to Wewahitchka in the newly established Gulf County and, in spite of protests that the area was too small to support a newspaper, formed the *Gulf County Breeze*.

Hanlon, a newspaper man since 1894, set his first type at the age of eight in the *Tifton Gazette*. A journeyman printer by the age of fifteen, Hanlon left his father's shop to make his own journalistic way. In varying capacities he was associated with many newspapers in Georgia and Florida, including papers in Tifton and Ocilla, Georgia, and Ocala, Gainesville, Tarpon Springs, and Titusville, Florida.

When my great-grandfather moved here just a year or so after Hanlon built the Breeze he began working with him, and the McKnights had been part of the Breeze's history ever since.

My dad's obsessed with bringing back the county's oldest and last independently owned newspaper—and not just because he has no retirement and needs it to survive, but because it's in his DNA, a part of his life for the entirety of his life, his family's legacy.

But it's not just that. It's how lost he's been since my mom died. Not just alone. Adrift. I see it so clearly in him, but have only recently begun to see how true it has been of me too—especially since her death had been so close to that of my wife's and son's.

—We need to cover it, he says. I'm thinking of doing a special edition of the *Breeze*.

His obsession, which includes some desperation, makes him preoccupied in a way that keeps him constantly in work mode and rarely if ever fully present. And makes me miss my dad.

—Think you should.

—I can't— Dad is saying, but stops as I turn to speak to Michael Lister as he leaves.

—Looking forward to your new novel, I say.

—Thanks man, he says. I really appreciate that.

—Well, I've already finished it, Dad says, and it's great. Your best yet I think.

—Thank you. That means a lot Mr. McKnight.

—You ever want to contribute anything to the paper, Dad says, you just let me know. We'd love to have you in it. A book review, an op-ed, anything.

—Will do. Thanks.

Lister leaves and Dad returns to what he was saying.

—I can't do it alone, Dad says. You help me a little extra the next few days?

—I'll do better than that.

—Oh yeah? How's that?

When I tell him, he sits in stunned silence for a moment, glazed doughnut suspended in midair between the paper plate on the table and his partially open mouth.

—And there's more big news coming today, I say. And I've got a scoop on it for you too.

—You're not fuckin' with me, are you? I'm too old to—

—It's no joke.

—You've been a busy boy, haven't you?

—You have no idea.

His eyes light up, twinkling brightly beneath his loose lids.

—Who is she?

—Huh?

—You only say you have no idea like that when there's a woman involved.

I smile. And it's not at all unlike the one I woke up with this morning. Or the one I had when I texted her a few minutes later.

Morning.
Morning yourself.
The big day is here. I hope it's great for you.
Already is thanks for texting me

A Certain Retribution

My pleasure. I know we disagree about what last night was, but whether it was 3 dates or none, I thoroughly enjoyed every moment of it.
Me too. Especially tasing the shit out of Donnie Ray.
Really? That was your favorite part?
Just sayin it stands out.
More than the kissing?
No not more than the kissing.
So why not say especially the way you kissed me?
Sorry.

—Well? Dad asks.
—Remember the Summers girl?
—The one with the eyes, yeah. Got a boys name.
—Reggie.
—Yeah. Reggie. Nice. When'd she get back in town?
—Yesterday. Day before.
—Working fast, aren't you?
—Or something like it.
—So, how you wanna proceed? We've got to get a website back up. Agree?

I nod, but before I can say anything my phone rings.
—Hello.
—Merrick. Sheriff Wilson. We're about to go into Dahl Roger's house. Thought you should be there.
—Just tell me when and where.
—Now. Our Town Road. House with all the cop cars. Can't miss it. Hurry. We can't wait long.

I hang up.
—Got to go, I say, dropping my napkin on the table. Meeting Robin at Dahl's. Says they're doing the first walkthrough.
—Says?
—I know he went into the car before I got there last night. I'll get with you later when we're done. If I get held up for any reason, you need to be at the city commissioners' meeting this afternoon.
—Really? Why?
—I'll explain later. I've got to go. They're waiting on me.

As I'm about to leave, the door dings again and Reggie

walks in with Rain.

—Hey, I say, stopping.

—Hey yourself.

We stand there for a moment just staring and smiling.

Rain wanders over to look at the doughnuts.

I turn back toward Dad.

—Reggie you remember my dad, Mac, don't you? Dad, Reggie Summers.

—Welcome home, young lady, he says.

—Thank you. How're you? I would've introduced y'all to Rain but . . . well . . . doughnuts.

—'Nough said.

I turn back toward her fully and lower my voice a little.

—How're you feelin'? I ask. Get any sleep?

—Not a lot. Someone kept me out late. Do I look sleepy?

—You look fresh as the morning. As beautiful too.

She smiles a smile that makes me want to grab her hand and run off with her.

—Thank you, she says.

Her voice has the same quality as the one following the first kiss and I can taste Trident Watermelon Twist and her warm mouth.

—Son, I thought you were in a hurry? Dad says from where he's still sitting at the table.

—No, I say. Not at all.

—Where're you headed?

—Dahl's. Sheriff and crime scene are about to go in.

—You better go, she says. We'll need to know what they find.

—Speaking of which, I say, I think I've discovered a little hiccup in your plan.

—Yeah? And what's that?

—It was nagging at me last night but I couldn't put my finger on it. Then as I was falling asleep . . .

—What?

—Even if you become the chief of police, Seven Springs is outside of the city limits, so Dahl's case will still be

A Certain Retribution

Robin's.
    She smiles.
    —What is it? I ask.
    —Just don't miss the commissioners' meeting.

    Dahl's little rundown house makes me sad.
    He had bought it on the cheap from the bank when it had been in foreclosure and now it is in foreclosure again.
    Not a particularly nice house to begin with, the previous tenants had trashed it before abandoning it and Dahl had done little to clean or fix it up since he'd been here.
    A HUD house built for a low-income family, the small brick home is serviceable and utilitarian, elevating function above form at every turn.
    A warped and bent garage door hangs perpetually partially open, molding junk and mess and trash spilling out the three-foot gap at the bottom.
    —Nice of you to join us, Skeeter Hamm, a longtime deputy and friend of Robin says.
    A half dozen deputies and techs are poised by the front door to enter, making a show of waiting for me.
    —Just come when you can, Skip Lester adds.
    —Ready? Robin says.
    I nod.
    —Next time call me before you actually want me here. It's a thing people do.
    —Get him gloved and let's go, Robin says.
    A male tech I don't recognize tosses me a pair of latex gloves.
    A female deputy in a blue tech suit steps up and unlocks the front door with a key held in a gloved hand.
    —Don't touch anything, Robin says.
    Inside we find a dwelling that seems simultaneously empty and cluttered.
    It is sparsely furnished—a random recliner in an

otherwise empty room, a dining table with only two chairs and no china cabinet or hutch, a bed but no dresser or chest of drawers—and yet virtually every inch of the cheap, stained carpet not part of the paths that run through it is covered with stacks of clothes and bags of disparate things and piles of papers and magazines, and more DVDs and weapons than I've ever seen outside of a retail outlet.

Shotguns, handguns, rifles, compound bows, knives—every make and manner imaginable in every single room in the house with no exceptions. Kitchen countertops with serrated survival knives, camo hunting knives, extreme tactical knives. Bedside tables with .45s and .38s. Piles of rifles on the dining table. Shotguns in every corner of every room.

—Damn, Skeeter says. Reckon this is the place to come when the apocalypse happens.

—No wonder he couldn't afford better clothes or a better car, Skip says.

—Or furniture, Skeeter adds.

—We're here to do a job, Robin says. Let's do it and get out of here. Priority is a suicide note or any evidence that might explain what happened last night.

—Yes sir, the male tech who'd thrown me the gloves says.

For the next hour or so I watch as they comb through the various rooms, examining all the material possessions Dahl Rogers had amassed during his short life.

The DVDs consist of military, action adventure, and horror movies, mostly low-budget B-movies and exploitation films. Interestingly, there's not a single porn title among them.

The magazines are mostly of the guns and ammo, survivalist, outdoors, hunting, and law enforcement variety.

An older model Dell desktop computer sits on the floor of an unfurnished bedroom.

Like the house itself, Dahl's computer reveals a sad, lonely man, gung-ho for gun rights and law enforcement, a decent man who doesn't appear to be involved in anything illegal. Paranoid perhaps, obsessive and excessive, but more bored than dangerous or depressed.

A Certain Retribution

—Wait, the female tech says, as she taps away on the computer's keyboard.

—What is it? Robin asks.

—There's . . . a . . . file . . . here. There's a file that's been deleted. Maybe nothing, but . . .

—What is it? Robin says. What's it say?

—I'll have to take it back to the lab and work on it. Might even have to get some help to recover it.

—Do it, Robin says. Bag it and tag it.

He steps to the door, looks down the hallway.

—Anybody else got anything?

No one did. Not really. A few other things are bagged and taken into evidence, but besides the deleted file, which might be nothing—a catalog of his weapons or movies, a resumé or unsent resignation letter—the house is, ironically, clean.

After getting Rain a couple of glazed doughnuts and a bottle of milk, which he wolfs down on the way to school, Reggie drops off the well-sugared lad for his second day of Wewa High and heads toward the old city hall building for the specially convened daytime meeting that will change everything.

Deciding to kill a little extra time so as not to arrive at city hall quite so many hours before the meeting, she turns onto Sesame Street to take a ride through Red Bull Island.

As much as Wewa is the same small town it always was, much has changed and she has to reacquaint herself with her onetime and once again home.

She had once loved this little town. Until what had been done to her she never saw herself leaving. After what had been done to her she couldn't get out fast enough, knowing she could never feel safe here again.

She intends to love this town again, to protect it, to protect herself, to feel safe, to make it truly safe for everyone, to find and punish those who had turned something sweet and sacred into something traumatic and horrific, to prevent what had happened to her from ever happening to another young person in this town.

Wewa is a beautiful town where something very ugly happened. She wants it to be just a beautiful town again. And it will be. She actually feels hopeful that it will.

She has driven less than half a mile when she sees the flashing lights in her rearview.

Quickly checking her speed and seatbelt and the placement of her car on the road, she determines she's not doing anything illegal.

She strains to see the deputy, deciding it must be Donnie Ray retaliating from last night, but between the bright lights and the glare on the windshield can't discern the driver.

She slows and pulls her car to the shoulder of the road and watches and waits.

Pulling her Taser out, she holds it down next to her seat.

For a long while the car just sits there, lights flashing, but eventually Donnie Ray gets out and swaggers toward her car.

I arrive early at the special city commissioners' meeting hoping to see Reggie before it begins.

Robin has returned to his office behind the courthouse in Port St. Joe, promising to notify me when he has anything on the missing file or when he sets up the interview with Donnie Ray.

The meeting is being held in the old two-story red-brick city hall building next to the fire station on Second Street.

The once busy building is now all but abandoned—used mostly for storage and commissioners' meetings since the city purchased the old county road department building and moved city hall there.

Rows of metal folding chairs atop thin dog-food-brown carpet surrounded by rough cypress plank walls. American flag and coffee pot up front. Framed photographs of the city's mayors. Slow-moving ceiling fans overhead. Empty desks in empty offices.

I look around but see no sign of Reggie.

There are very few people present. If she were here I would see her.

I walk back outside and am standing on the front porch of the old city hall building looking at the ancient fire truck parked out in front of the open bay of the fire department when Dad pulls up.

—Wasn't sure if you were going to make it back for the meeting, he says when he walks up.

—Finished at Dahl's a little sooner than I expected. Came straight here. Was about to call you.

—No problem. Wanted to be here anyway. See what the big revelations are.

I nod.

—Turn up anything at Dahl's? he asks.

I shake my head.

—Not really, I say. No way to know whether they went in and removed anything before I got there.

—Got to think it's a good possibility with Robin Wilson in charge. Reggie inside?

—She hasn't made it yet.

He glances at his watch and we fall silent a moment.

Eventually his gaze drifts across the way to the old *Breeze* building.

—We should buy that building and bring the *Breeze* home, he says.

The small building directly across Second Street from the old city hall and fire department was home to the *Breeze* for a few decades, back when it actually required a printing press. Now the entire process requires only a computer or two, with the actual printing being outsourced.

Prior to that, the *Breeze* office was located in the bottom of a two-story wooden building that C.F. Hanlon and his family lived in the upstairs of, on Osceola Street—behind the old city hall building we're standing in front of now. Hanlon spent many hours in a swing on the front porch of the building battin' the breeze, which is where the name for the paper, the *Gulf County Breeze* and his column *Battin' the Breeze* originated. Except for a two year period in the early 1930s when the newspaper changed hands temporarily, Hanlon operated the *Breeze* from 1925 until 1953 and never missed an issue.

In January 1954, due to failing health, C.F. Hanlon sold the paper to young Navy Lieutenant Edward A. Bandjough. Still on active duty, Bandjough delayed his first issue until June 1954. In the interim, J.C. Hanlon, son of C.F. Hanlon, and my grandfather J.M. McKnight operated the *Breeze*, which they had been doing since the time of C.F.'s illness.

New to the newspaper business, Bandjough taught himself how to operate and repair his own equipment by studying the manuals. Visitors to his shop recall that the manual for each piece of equipment hung above it.

In December 1954, the two-story wooden *Breeze* office on Osceola burned down and the *Breeze* was temporarily located in the Connell Water Works building on Lake Grove Road near where the water tower now stands.

Eventually, the *Breeze* moved into the building directly across from us now and Bandjough and McKnight installed new equipment, including electrical equipment, a Linotype machine, and a hot lead press.

We barely have a paper. We certainly don't need the building across Second Street or any other, but Dad is a dreamer, not very good at business. He's trying to save his family's small-town paper, trying to resurrect it to the point of mere survival. Buying a building is the last thing he needs to do, but a misguided sense of nostalgia would lead him to try if he thought he could.

—Let's make sure we have a *Breeze* before we think about anything else.

—You're right, but wouldn't it be cool? Maybe we could even get the old Linotype machine and printing press back and make a museum or something. We could even put out certain special editions that we lay out on the old Linotype machine and print on the old press. Mix new media and old. Be an amazing place for us to work together, wouldn't it?

I nod.

—It would, I say.

Right now the *Breeze* office is in his garage and I understand the appeal of what he's describing, but it's so outside of what's even possible, and he's always wasted so much time, energy, and money in pursuit of similar pipe dreams and schemes, that it dredges up some old anger I have at him.

—Wonder if we could get some sort of historical grant or something? he says.

—If you want my help with the paper you've got it, I say. If you want to try to buy buildings or make museums or work on historical grants, then I'll leave you to it and I'll do something else.

He stares at me in stunned silence for a moment.

—No, you're right, he says eventually. Sorry. I get caught up in . . . Let's concentrate on getting the paper back on its feet. I won't . . . I'll stop . . . I'll take off my entrepreneurial hat for a while. Promise.

I nod and we stand in a slightly strained silence for a moment.

—I'm gonna go on in and take a look around. See you inside.

—Be in in a minute. Gonna call Reggie. Make sure she's okay.

After he's gone I do. She doesn't answer and I don't leave a message. I wait a few more minutes then try her again, this time leaving a message when she doesn't answer.

I am about halfway through the message when a call comes in from a number I don't recognize. Given all that's going on I click over and take the call.

And I'm glad I do.

—Merrick, Reggie says.

I can tell immediately something is wrong. Her voice in tight and tense, panic at its jagged edges.

—Are you okay? I ask. Where are you?

—No. I'm not. I've been arrested. I'm in the Gulf County jail.

—Hey Merrick, Robin says in his overly friendly and familiar voice. What're you doing here?

—Need to talk to you, I say.

—Well come on in, he says.

I do, closing the door behind me.

His office is cleaner, more organized and nicer than I expect. It has the usual plaques, awards, and citations, the community and family photos, the mounted animal heads, but there's not a single thing in the room that doesn't need to be.

Just as I was crossing the old railroad tracks coming into town, Dad had called and given me the news from the special city commissioners' meeting. He was surprised as I knew he would be, but he also surprised me with another decision the commissioners had made.

—Everyone's wondering why she's not here, he had said. Should I tell them?

—Let them know that she's been detained and that I've gone to pick her up. Don't say anything else. Let me see if I can get it sorted out first.

—Ten-four, he had said.

I am hoping the news he had given me can be used as leverage with Robin.

—Have a seat, Robin is saying. What can I do for you? This about Dahl's case?

I shake my head.

—No, I say, though I've been impressed by how professional your department is in conducting the investigation.

He nods and smiles.

—I knew you would be, he says. That's why I wanted an objective outsider observing and reporting on it. Let the people know the FDLE investigation is as ridiculous as it is unfounded.

I nod.

—So if it's not about Dahl, he says, what can I do for you?

—You can release Reggie Summers.

A Certain Retribution

—Oh she will be soon. She'll go before the judge after lunch and can make bail shortly thereafter. I'd say she'll be a free woman by two o'clock.

—No, I mean let her go now, I say. Drop all charges.

—Merrick, you know I can't do that. Even if I wanted to. That's the very thing FDLE is wanting me to do. I remember Reggie from high school and I liked her back then—as far as it goes, but she's always had an attitude problem. Always looking for a fight. Something like this was inevitable. And I bet if you look into her past you'll see a pattern of behavior and possibly other altercations. She's made her bed. Now she's gonna have to lie in it. Least for a while. And this ain't no little thing she's accused of. It's a serious crime.

—What is?

—Assault on a law enforcement officer.

—Donnie Ray Kemp? I say.

He nods.

—Robin, I say. You can't be serious.

—Why can't I?

—You don't really believe she assaulted Donnie Ray.

—Deputy Kemp, he says. And yes I do.

—With as careful as you're trying to be right now it surprises me you're sabotaging yourself like this.

—I'm afraid you've lost me, Merrick. I don't follow.

—Then let me 'splain it. Front page of tomorrow's papers. Headline reads something like Deputy Suspected in Cop's Death Arrests Woman Who Came to Victim's Aid.

—Huh?

—Or something like that. That's not very good, but you get the point. Last night Donnie Ray, drunk off his ass, harasses and assaults and threatens Dahl. I try to help and he does the same to me. Reggie steps in and saves us both by taking on Donnie Ray herself. A few hours later Dahl is dead, and a few hours after that Donnie's arrested Reggie.

—Merrick, he says, his voice full of disapproval and correction, you're spinning that and you know it.

—That's no spin at all. Just facts. But believe me it will be spun—and not just by the papers tomorrow but the TV news programs this evening.

Tiny fissures in his facade begin to show.

—But wait, I say. There's more. A lot more. There's a much larger context. This is happening in a department already operating under a cloud of suspicion because of an FDLE investigation.

He frowns and shakes his head—in frustration, even resignation, but not disagreement.

—And, I add, this happens on the same day as the City of Wewahitchka votes to end its contract with the Gulf County Sheriff's Department and institute their own police department again.

The look on his face—shock, sickness, denial, fear—says it all. He had no idea.

—Did they?

I nod.

—In a special meeting still going on at the moment, I say. But there's more.

He gives me a look that says he's scared to ask but wants to know.

—The person Donnie Ray arrested is the one who has just been appointed police chief of Wewa.

His mask and manipulative demeanor are suddenly gone.

—They made Reggie fuckin' Summers chief of police?

I nod.

—Think about it, Robin. Think long and hard. Dahl is accusing you and your deputies of corruption. Donnie Ray threatens and attempts to assault him. Reggie intervenes and stops him. Then Dahl is found dead. And the person about to take over the investigation into his death is arrested by the prime suspect.

—Okay, okay. I see what you're saying. I'll have her released. But you're wrong about one thing. She's not taking over my investigation. Seven Springs is outside the city limits. Even with her becoming chief she won't get the case.

—Actually, I say, that's the other thing the commissioners voted on. They extended the city limits to include Seven Springs just so it would be her case. It already is her case. Was before I walked in here.

—You okay? I ask.
She shakes her head.
—Just get me away from these motherfuckers as fast as possible.
I drive her away from the jail and the motherfuckers like Robin Wilson and Donnie Ray Kemp and over to the No Name Cafe on Reid Avenue.
She is visibly upset, the anger and frustration and humiliation emanating from her red hot lava core palpable.
A slight tremor causes her hands to shake, her mouth is pursed and she is worrying with her lips, biting at them, and her erratic breaths come out in angry bursts and huffs and sighs.
—How much was bail? she asks. Why didn't I go before the judge?
—No bail.
—What? How?
—I convinced Robin it was in his best interest to drop the charges and let you go.
—How?
I tell her.
She nods appreciatively and begins to calm down, the tension in her body slowly dissipating as she unclenches.
—So the commissioners did it even without me there? What was the vote?
—Four to one. You're the chief of police of the best little town in the world. A town that is a little bigger now.
—That passed too? The Dahl Rogers case is mine?
—It is.
—I should get back to Wewa. Is the meeting still going on?
—No, I say. Dad said it's over. I had him tell them your car broke down and that you were so sorry you couldn't be present but that you were going to give all you had to be the

best chief possible.
   —Thank you.
   —And you need to eat and relax for a minute before we head back.
   She smiles.
   —You're right, she says.
   The No Name Cafe is part deli, part coffee house, part bookstore, and part gift shop. The environment is perfect for her to unwind and us to talk while grabbing a bite and browsing the books.
   We sit at a table in the front and can see the traffic on Reid, the midday sun large and looming overhead, brightening and warming and healing and glinting.
   When the food arrives she thanks me again.
   —I'm counting this as a date, I say.
   She smiles and looks more like the girl from last night again.
   —I think you should.
   We eat in silence for a few moments, looking around at the books and gifts and the orange-and-black Halloween decorations.
   —You seem better now, I say.
   She looks up and seems to think about it, her stunning eyes catching the light from the window and becoming even more mesmerizing, then nods slowly, thoughtfully.
   —What'd they do to you?
   —Wasn't so much what they did as the threat they represent. I have a history with them. To be put in that position . . . powerless . . . completely under their control . . . It's like someone with PTSD being put back in the situation that caused it.
   I nod.
   —I'm so sorry, I say. You keep saying *they*.
   —Robin and Donnie Ray. A few others that work there too, but those are the only ones I saw.
   —And this goes back to . . .
   —High school.
   —What's the threat? I ask. What'd they do to you?

—Listen, Merrick. I remember you as a very sweet boy and you've been so nice since we bumped into each other again. It's been so . . . refreshing. I mean . . . well, you know . . . but the truth is we just re-met, are just getting reacquainted . . .

I nod again.

—I'm just . . . I don't want to talk about it.

—Then we won't.

—Really? she asks. Do you understand?

—I do, I say. Completely.

—Thank you.

Over the next few weeks my life pretty much went back to the way it was before Reggie came into it again.

As she was settling into her new position, setting up an office, responding to the needs of the town, investigating Dahl Rogers's death, I was helping Dad with the new and improved *Gulf County Breeze*. While she was raising Rain and taking care of her mom, I was working with Kevin on socialization and Casey on career choices.

I didn't see much of Reggie at all. And I missed her. More than I ever thought I would. I kept up with what she was doing. We talked at least a little every day. And though the conversations were meaningful, even relationship building, they only made me want to see her, to be with her, all the more.

Today I call her with the intention of seeing her.

—I want to see you, I say when she answers her phone. Today. Tonight at the latest.

—I'm driving Mom home from the doctor right now, then I've got to go clean out the jail cell in the old city hall and get it ready in case I ever need a temporary holding cell. And then I have to patrol tonight.

Since she's a police force of one, she mostly works nights, patrolling our small town in her own vehicle until the city purchases one. Her office is in the only building in town with a jail cell, the old city hall. It's rarely used—maybe once or twice a month for meetings—so she'll have the entire building to herself.

—If you don't want to see me that's one thing, I say. But if you do, we can work it out.

—I'm just real busy, she says. Got so much going on.

I wait but that's all she says so I attempt to exit gracefully, and hang up the phone frustrated.

I try to go back to work on the *Breeze* website but I'm too disappointed, too raw from the rejection. I get up from my desk in Dad's garage and walk outside.

Wewahitchka's water eyes, Alice and Julia, are separated by a hundred yards or so on which are a few houses and Highway 22. Dad lives in an old family home on Lake Julia.

I walk down to the water's edge beneath the moss-draped cypress trees and stare out at Julia.

The mid-October day is sunny and bright, but breezy and a bit chilly. Julia seems agitated, the wind-distressed surface of her waters choppy and sparkly at the same time.

Every time Reggie and I get close, or seem to be beginning to, she backs off or pushes me away. It's subtle but undeniable. Do I hang in there? See if she will eventually open up more and give us a chance at something, or is this who she is? Has she lived with armor so long, has it become so integrated into who she is, that it's part of her?

Thought you had sworn off women for a while anyway? Didn't you say after what happened with Regan that you knew you needed to be alone for a while?

I have been. It's been a long while now.

My phone rings. It's Reggie.

—Sorry, she says. My relationship with my mom is . . . complicated. I can't talk about stuff like that in front of her.

—Stuff like what? It's not like we were talking about sex.

—Anything. I can't really talk about much of anything in front of her.

—Okay, I say. Well, thanks for letting me know. I appreciate you calling back to tell me.

—Sounds like you're hanging up, she says. Get your little panties out of a wad and tell me how we can see each other

A Certain Retribution

with our schedules the way they are.
—I can help you work on the holding cell, I say.
—Really?
—Sure.
—Hell you must really want to see me.
—I do. It was the first thing out of my mouth when you answered the phone.
—Just put it out there, Merrick. Don't hold back.

When I arrive at the old city hall at the corner of Osceola and Second, Reggie is already busy removing boxes from the two cells in the back to the large room upstairs.

After saying hey and giving her a quick hug I jump in and begin helping her, grabbing the nearest box I can find.

The ancient gray iron bar cells are bolted to the floor and walls. Inside, beneath a single bare bulb light fixture, the dungeon-like jail cells consist of a bare concrete floor and peeling plaster walls revealing the rough ash-colored stones behind.

One cell is empty except for cardboard boxes on the floor. The other actually has metal shelves lining the walls, filled with file folders and office supplies and big black ledger books and city records and a hundred other random dust-covered papers and boxes and objects.

—These are some wicked badass-looking cells just to be used for storage, I say.

She stops and stares at me, eyebrows raised, expression questioning, challenging.
—That's it? she asks.
—What?
—Just get straight to work?
—Whatta you want me to do? I hugged you and—
—You know what I mean. That's a hug you'd give your sister.
—Whatta you want from me? I say.

—To be your warm, sweet self.
—No matter how you act?
—Yes, she says, a small smile dancing at the corners of her mouth.
I laugh.
The answer is unexpected and refreshing. To offer no defense and come out and say exactly what she means is as disarming as it is endearing.
—Sometimes you act so interested in something with me, then others . . .
—Yep.
—That's not easy.
—Nope.
—Okay, I say, and step over and kiss her and hug her again—longer this time and far less sisterly.
—That's more like it, she says.
—I've missed you, I say. I'm glad to see you.
She smiles but doesn't say anything.
—See? I say. Like that. I say things like those to you and you don't say anything . . .
—Yep.
—It's a lot to ask.
—It is, she says. And if you want to drop freight and haul ass now, nobody'd blame ya. But I hope you don't. I'm actually open to something with you, Merrick. That's something I haven't been since before Rain was born.
—He's sixteen.
—Exactly.
—You haven't had a relationship in sixteen years?
—I haven't had much of anything, she says. I've been raising my son. Alone. But I've been involved with a loser or two. What I'm sayin' is I'm open to something real with you and the only reason I am even a little open—and that's all it is right now—is because it's you, because of how you are. And when you act other than your kind sweet self it doesn't help.
—All I was was a little more platonic than I really feel, I say. A little less warm, but hell, I'm here helping you move shit and—

A Certain Retribution

—I know.
—Well?
—I'm a mess. I'm no good at relationships. You should run. Now. But if you're gonna stay, if you're gonna try to actually be with someone like me, you have to remember that I'm insecure and have low self-esteem and I get rejected real easy, can get my feelin's hurt from something as little as a sisterly hug. I'm a lot of work. And I'm probably not worth it. But them's the breaks. Now you know—or actually I bet you already did—so make up your mind with full knowledge of the whole catastrophe that is me and either—

I pull her in and kiss her again, hugging and holding her emphatically.

—You're so . . . I adore who and how you are, I say. You're so honest and unassuming and . . . Sign me up for the full ride. I'm in.

—Like insecure girls, do you?
—Least one I can think of.
—Well, okay then. Help her clear out some boxes to make room for the bad guys.

Which we do, making a million tiring trips up the old wooden steps in the front to the open auditorium upstairs to place the clutter from the cells alongside the clutter of Christmas decorations and water-damaged boxes and antiquated office machinery already up there.

When she returns to the cell after finding a place for the final box, I'm waiting for her. Grabbing her, I press her up against the wall, lean in and kiss her hard.

She kisses back just as hard and our passion and exploration of each other intensifies.

—Ready for your initiation, new fish? I say in my best, baddest inmate voice.

—I think I'm gonna like my new cellmate, she says. When is lights out?

We make out some more. And some more.

—Does this count as a date? I ask.
—Tryin' to decide if you can cop a feel or not?

Instead of answering her, I reach up under her shirt and

down inside her bra and gently cup her breast in my hand.

When she tries to say something, I kiss her so I can't hear what it is.

—You should've let me talk, she says when I pull back slightly. I was gonna tell you to pinch the nipple, but you—

I sense someone is there the moment before he speaks.

—What's this? Robin Wilson says.

We turn to see him standing in the doorway.

He nods to himself and makes an expression that says he's just confirmed something he's suspected, then shakes his head at us.

—Merrick, I expect this from a . . . from someone like her, but you? Never suspected it out of you.

—Really Robin? You didn't think I liked girls?

—I'm talkin' about betrayal. I'm talkin' about conspiracy.

—You're talkin' nonsense is what you're talkin', Reggie says.

—Don't even try to pretend, he says. I know why you're here. I know what you're up to. But you, he adds, turning his attention back to me, you've joined the crusade to take me down. After I brought you into my investigation. After I opened up everything to you so you could see firsthand how good a sheriff I am, how good my department is, how I had nothing to do with Dahl's death.

I start to say something but he stops me.

—Save it, he says. I actually stopped by to offer this crazy bitch an olive branch, but—

—Call me a crazy bitch again and see if I don't stomp a mud hole in the middle of you, Reggie spits, rage instantly emanating from her.

I can't tell whether it's a deliberate act meant to send a message or a subconscious, almost autonomic response, but his hand drifts over to the butt of his holstered .45 and lingers there for the rest of the conversation.

He shakes his head and lets out a mean little laugh, all attempts at his soft sweet-voiced manipulation gone.

—You need to go, I say.

—I'll go when I get good and goddamn ready to and not

a second before. Don't you forget who I am.

—Oh I know who the hell you are, Reggie says. I know what you are.

—I came by to remind you that I'm the sheriff of Gulf County, which means I'm the chief law-enforcement officer for the entire county, and that Wewa is in Gulf County, which means I'm the chief law-enforcement officer for Wewa. To tell you that I had absolutely nothing to do with Dahl's death. Far as I can tell he killed himself. And to offer my department's help as you try to play police chief for a little while. But now . . . now I've got a different message. Watch yourselves. I mean you harm. I'm gonna bring you both down hard. Swear you that. I wouldn't leave the city limits if I was you—unless it's to run away from here again like you both done before, but this time not to ever come back.

Early the next morning, I am standing at the front window, staring through the lace curtain at the deputy car parked across the street, when Casey pads sleepily into the living room behind me and plops down onto the couch. Her shoulder-length blond hair stands out on one side, her green eyes barely visible sleepy slits.

—What're you doin' up so early? she asks.

—Could ask you the same thing.

—I have a test, she says.

Since coming to live with me, Casey has been back in college, finishing her AA at Gulf Coast State College then transferring to the Panama City branch campus of Florida State University.

—You? she asks.

—I'm being tested, I say with a smile.

—Huh?

—Nothin'. How are you?

—Sleepy as shit, but otherwise not bad. I'd ask how you are but it's obvious.

—It is?
—You're happy.
—I am.
—Aren't you? You've met someone, haven't you? It's that kind of happy.

I smile.

—I have, yes. Someone I sort of went to school with.
—Sort of?
—She was a few grades behind me.
—Not too many I hope.
—No. She's four years younger than me.
—What's she like?
—Unlike anyone I've ever dated.
—Yeah?
—She's a cowgirl. Country girl.
—Every girl around here is a country girl.

I laugh.

—She's country as fuck, I say. Told the sheriff she'd stomp a mud hole in the middle of him last night.
—That why there's a police car parked out front?
—The sheriff is not a good guy, I say.
—No kidding, Captain Obvious.
—I wasn't finished, but what do you know about him?
—I know men, she says. I know his type. I know just by watching him operate.

After her biological dad died and before I got her back, Casey had worked for a short while as a stripper at a club in Panama City.

—He drugged and raped a girl I go to school with, she says.
—Did she report it? Is she—
—She couldn't prove anything. They were on a date. Even if they had done a rape kit, he'd just say it was consensual. She didn't even bother, but when she heard about the investigation she contacted FDLE and they interviewed her.
—Good, I say. What I was saying is that Reggie and I are on his bad list. We're gonna need to be extra careful for a while. Look out for Kevin. Stay close. Communicate really well about

where you're going and what you're doing.

The truth is after what happened to Casey a few years back—being abducted and assaulted and held against her will after being Miss Thunder Beach—she stays pretty close anyway, and always lets me know where she is and when I can expect her home. It's only recently that she's been willing to go out without me. I hope this doesn't set her back.

—Okay? I ask.

—You don't have to tell me twice. 'Course I don't know how you gonna get any with me and Kevin around all the time.

I laugh.

—Where there's a will . . . I say.

—Merrick, it's really good to see you happy. You deserve it.

—Are you?

—I am, actually. Not as happy as you. I ain't in love or any shit like that, but, yeah, I'm very happy. And that has a lot to do with you. That's why it makes me happy that you're happy.

—Thank you.

—And why I hope we all live long enough for you to enjoy it a while.

—Just ignore it, Reggie's mom, Sylvia, is saying.

It's her response to Robin having deputies following us.

It's late. The house is quiet and dim.

The three of us are sitting at their dinner table, eating eggs and bacon and toast. Rain is fast asleep in his room. Outside, in the corner lot across Byrd Parker Drive, a deputy sits in his car watching the mobile home, window partially rolled down, cigarette smoke rising from it.

Reggie has prepared the meal in the middle of the night because Sylvia said not only did she feel like eating but wanted to try to do it at the table.

—It's harassment, Reggie says. We've talked about this before, Mom. A bully won't stop because you ignore him.

You've always taken the wrong approach. Did Dad stop? Did your dad? What about what Becky and poor little Lexi Lee are going through right now?

Becky is Reggie's older sister, Lexi Lee her niece. I don't know what they're going through right now but I have wondered why, since they live in town, they aren't helping with Sylvia, why I haven't even seen them.

—I just think you make things worse when you—

—What? Reggie says, challenging. When you stand up for yourself? When you refuse to be a victim?

The level and intensity of Reggie's anger goes far beyond the current conversation. It's far more about the past than the present, far more about her complicated relationship with her mom and her history with Robin than what's happening right now, and it reminds me of what Faulkner said about the past not only not being dead but not even being past.

—I'm sorry, Sylvia says. I shouldn't've said anything. I just hate to see you get so worked up. It's not good for you.

—And repressing everything is?

Her raised eyebrows expression and the little way she indicates her mom with her hand conveys her message as clearly as if she had come out and said it. Her mom's passivity and repression has led to her disease.

—I'm ready for bed, her mom says. My eyes were bigger than my stomach. Thanks for cooking it for me, Regg. Hope it wasn't too much trouble.

—Sorry, I just—

Reggie's phone rings.

—I've got to take this. Sorry.

—Merrick can help me to bed.

I can and I do, walking sideways down the narrow hall while lending a supportive hand to the slowly shuffling Sylvia.

I enjoy spending time with Sylvia. She is so different from my mom and her presence often brings out the worst in Reggie, but being around her makes the mom-sized hole in me recede a bit.

Reggie has stepped away from the table and is in the far corner of the open room but we can hear much of what she is saying.

—She's so angry with me, Sylvia says.

—Over?

—I'm sure she's right . . . We're just so different. Perhaps I have been bullied my whole life. Maybe that is why I'm sick. I just . . . I don't know. I know I've let her down.

She continues like that until I have her in the bed and am pulling up the covers around her.

—You're good for her, Merrick, she says. I know she's not easy, but she's worth it. Hang in there and help her, would you?

—I will, I say. Don't plan on going anywhere.

I start to ease out of the room but she stops me.

—You're such kind, good man, she says. That seems so rare these days but that can't be right, can it? Can't be as rare as it seems.

—Thank you, I say. It's too rare. That's for sure.

—I was so sorry to hear about the accident, she says. When it happened I remember it was two months to the day that I had been at your mom's funeral.

I nod.

—Dark days, I say, images of myself being unable or unwilling to get out of bed several days in a row streaking through the night sky of my mind.

Feelings of guilt and despair, true deep despair, sink heavily into my stomach as I recall the sad, lost, lonely man who ate too little, drank too much, did very little—except lose Casey and Kevin.

—And yet . . . she begins but breaks off.

—Ma'am?

—I worry about Reggie, she says. How were you able to keep that darkness from getting into you?

—I wasn't, I say. Not entirely.

—But now you're so—

—I've worked hard at gettin' it back out again.

—And you've succeeded.

—Not entirely, I say.

—That was my computer guy, Reggie says when I walk back into the trailer's great room. He recovered the file. On his way over with it.

—That's good.

—How is she? she asks, as she starts to clear the plates from the table.

—Seems fine. Think she fell asleep before I was out of the room. You were a little hard on her, weren't you?

She stops what she's doing, dropping a fork onto a plate loudly, and looks at me angrily.

—What'd you say?

—Just seemed a little ironic.

She squints in incomprehension.

—What does?

—Felt like you were bullying her about not letting herself be bullied.

—Oh, is that what it felt like? I think it's time for you to go. I've got work to do.

—Reggie.

She doesn't respond.

—I question something you do and you kick me out?

—You don't know anything about it, she says.

—I've been asking you to tell me.

—After you sided with her? You kidding?

—I didn't side with her. Sorry if it seemed that way.

She goes back to clearing the table and I begin to help her.

We work together for a while in silence, cleaning the kitchen, washing the dishes, putting away the food.

—Sorry, she says eventually.

—Me too. I shouldn't've said anything.

—No, you were right. She just makes me so . . .

—What's going on with Becky and Lexi Lee? I ask.

—Becky married a version of our dad—an alcoholic asshole who controls everything they do. Eric Layton.

A Certain Retribution

Remember him? They called him Air Prick in school 'cause there was nothing there.

—Little guy, I say. Short, small. Paranoid and pouty.

—That's the one. Pansy ass little tattletale that always seemed like he was about to cry.

—That's who Becky wound up with?

—We're not known for picking winners. He's a mean little drunk. They're rarely allowed out of his house. He terrifies poor little Lexi. Refuses to let them help with Mom.

—Y'all keep saying little Lexi Lee, but isn't she . . .

—She's nearly two years older than Rain. Seventeen soon to be eighteen. She's just small and frail—seems even more so because of how beat down he makes her.

—Last time I saw her I remember thinking how much she looks like you.

—That's what everybody says. That she's the spitting image of me, but the truth is she's smaller than I ever was. And I may have been insecure and kind of sad but I was never beat down.

I smile.

—No you weren't. And still aren't. And thank God for that.

Adam Ake, Reggie's computer guy, is a tall, early twenties young man with black hair, a quick smile, and the laid back demeanor of a surfer or stoner or mellow musician. He's in all black—jeans, T-shirt, and flip flops.

—You're not cold? Reggie asks him when she opens the door to him.

—Little. Forgot to grab my jacket before I left. Didn't feel like going back for it once I got outside.

—You know Merrick?

—Everybody knows Merrick. He's in the paper like every other day.

—How's it going, man? I say.

—Yeah. Not bad. You?
—Good.
—Cool.
—Hey. I just had a thought. I've got this amazing and beautiful stepdaughter who needs a nice guy to take her out. Can't believe I didn't think of you before.
—How tall is she?
—Five-five. Why?
—I only go for short women.
—Five-five short enough?
—It's a joke, man. I'm like six-four and my girlfriend's like four-nine.
—That'd be funny if the punchline wasn't that you had a girlfriend.
—I'll let you know if anything changes. You're talking about Casey, right? She's a straight-up fox.
—So, Reggie says, whatcha got for me?
—This is some serious shit. Should I be worried? How dangerous is it? I mean, downloading movies and shit is one thing . . . but this is . . . real . . . this is heavy, man.
—You're fine, she says. What is it?
—This.
He pulls a single sheet of paper out of a file folder and hands it to her.
—Oh sweet Jesus Christ almighty, she says.
—Exactly, Adam says. See?
—What? I say. What is it?
She begins reading.
—If I am found dead it's because Robin Wilson or one of his men killed me. He is a bad corrupt cop and should not wear the badge. If I had any balls at all I would shoot him in the face. I am going to turn over evidence to FDLE. If he finds out, I am dead. If he doesn't pull the trigger himself and he probably won't, it will be Donnie Ray Kemp, Skeeter Hamm, Skip Lester, Jason Cox, or Wayne Weeks. No matter how it looks, they did it. I hope I can take them down before they get me but—
—That's it, Adam says. That's all that was in it. Just

stops.
—You sure there's nothing else? Reggie asks.
—Positive. I went through his whole hard drive. That's it.
—Well, it's enough, she says. Thank you.
She turns to me.
I nod.
—We've got him, she says.
—I'm not sure that's what it means, I say, but it's helpful.
—Is it for real? Adam asks. Did the sheriff really kill him?
—Not a word to anyone, Reggie says.
—Who would I tell? I don't want anyone to know I know. Hell, I don't want to know. Wish I didn't.
—Can you tell when the file was deleted? I ask. I bet they went into Dahl's and did it long before they ever called me.
—If that's true, Reggie says, then why point out a file is missing?
—Maybe the tech wasn't involved.
—The thing is, Adam says, the file was deleted just a short while after it was created.
He withdraws another sheet of paper from the file folder and hands it to Reggie.
—This is days before he died, she says.
—Most likely scenario is that he started writing it, stopped in the middle, then deleted it, I say.
—That's what I'd guess, Adam says.
—Just 'cause the bastard didn't delete it, Reggie says, don't mean he didn't kill him.

A few days later, Reggie is putting the finishing touches on her office when Maureen Evans walks in.
Closing the white wooden door with the opaque glass square, Maureen hands Reggie her card and sits down in the old, uncomfortable metal folding chair in front of her desk.
—I'm Maureen Evans from FDLE Executive

Investigations.

—Sorry about the seat, Reggie says. I'm having to use what I can find. Just gettin' set up.

Maureen looks around the small room, glancing at the cypress plank walls, the thin brown carpet, and the old wooden desk that was already in the room when Reggie chose the office.

As Maureen looks at their surroundings, Reggie looks at her. The deep redness of her auburn hair is as severe as the pale whiteness of her skin. She is a little too thin in a bony, pointy way with too much makeup poorly applied.

—It's not bad, she says. Got the entire building to yourself?

—I do.

—Hard to beat that.

—It is.

—How're you settling into your new position? Can't be easy?

—Never been one to go for easy.

—Probably true of every woman in law enforcement. Still, to start a department from scratch and under the circumstances. . .

—It's not from scratch. This desk was already in here. Found the chair upstairs. Got two ancient jail cells in the back and a radar gun from the fifties upstairs.

—An embarrassment of riches.

—Ain't it, though?

They are silent a moment.

—Get you some coffee or anything? Reggie asks.

—I'm fine. Thanks.

—Then down to business?

—No reason not to. You notified our office about a document you found.

—I did, but before I show you mine, whatta you say you show me yours?

Maureen looks puzzled.

—Tell me about your division and your investigation.

—Executive investigations mostly handles cases involving public officials. If a crime is alleged or the governor orders it or by a joint resolution by the Florida House and Senate.

—Which is the case with Sheriff Wilson?

—The first two. We received several allegations against Sheriff Wilson so we were investigating, but eventually the governor ordered it too. He appointed Wilson when John Milton died in office and was maybe a little slow to do it, but he eventually saw the . . . ah . . . political expediency.

—What kind of crimes and wrongdoings is he accused of?

—Wilson was a deputy before his appointment—had been for a long time—so we're following inquiries that go way back.

—Okay, but what? What's he accused of?

—Honestly? About everything a person in his position could be. Official misconduct—illegal behavior while using his position of authority. Your basic abuse-of-power type crimes. Obstruction of justice. There are several allegations of that for interfering with an investigation or the normal process of the law—everything from fixing tickets for friends to halting investigations of the guilty to conducting harassing investigations of the innocent to retaliate for perceived or actual slights. To actual destruction of physical evidence—tampering with or destroying everything from evidence collected at crime scenes to shredding of official paperwork.

—And?

—That's not enough?

—Is he guilty?

—The investigation is ongoing, Maureen says. I can't comment on—

—Hell, I know he's guilty. Everyone in these parts does. He's corrupt as fuck. Always has been. What I'm asking you is are you going to be able to make a case?

—That's not as easy as you might think, but I'm cautiously optimistic that justice will be served.

—Well, before you serve it, you might want to add murder to the list of charges, Reggie says as she opens the file folder on her desk and hands her the printout from Dahl's computer.

After Maureen Evans leaves, Reggie walks out of the old city hall building and over to the Express Lane convenience store at the town's only traffic light for a F'real Mint Chip Milkshake.

As she walks in the store's front door, she nods to the gaunt, morose man sitting at the table on the front porch of the store.

It's not until she has mixed her milkshake and is walking back up to the front to pay for it that she realizes who it is.

When she walks back outside, he is gone.

Quickly crossing the parking lot, she looks up and down Main Street attempting to find him.

At first she doesn't see him, but then a movement catches her eye.

Heading north, he's in front of what is now Centennial Bank, which she will always think of as Wewa State Bank, about to enter Lake Alice Park.

She races down the sidewalk on the opposite side, crosses the street, and catches up to him under the pavilion in the park.

—Allen?

He turns toward her.

—Hey Reggie, he says softly, his voice, like his demeanor, low and weak.

One year her senior, he looks at least twenty. Unshaven. Unkempt. Unwashed. If he were to tell her he is homeless it wouldn't surprise her.

His clothes, soiled jeans, worn sneakers, a too-big T-shirt, and a NASCAR hoodie, look saggy and slept in.

His early gray hair hangs down over his sad eyes in desperate need of washing and cutting, and his sun-damaged skin is wrinkled and leathery.

Is this really the kind, charming boy who took me to prom?

A Certain Retribution

He might as well be a stranger.
—Heard you were back in town, he says.
—How are you?
—Good. You know. Living the dream.
She smiles courteously.
—How long's it been? he asks.
—Since school, right? I came back for a couple of the reunions but never bumped into you.
—I avoid all that sort of thing.
—What're you up to?
—Same old. You know.
—Where do you live?
—Down by the school, he says, and when he's not more specific she suspects he's in the projects if he's anywhere at all.
—Are you okay?
—Never would've believed you'd come back, he says.
—Me either, but Mom is sick and I have a few scores to settle.
—You serious?
—About which?
—The scores.
She nods.
—Heard you was a cop or something, he says.
—Police chief in a department of one.
They are silent a moment, the breeze blowing off Lake Alice and up the small slope into the pavilion cool and refreshing.
—How can I help you, Allen? she asks.
—Huh?
—What can I do for you? What do you need?
—I don't understand. Whatta you mean?
—You seem so . . .
—I'm fine. Just worry about yourself. Why'd you come back? What good will it do? You got out, got away from them. Why would you come back?
—I told you.
He shakes his head and looks away.
—Are you punishing yourself for what happened? she

asks.

—I should've never let...

—What happened, happened to you as much as me.

She's never really realized just how profoundly and devastatingly true that is before this moment, before seeing him like this.

—You're not to blame, she says. It wasn't your fault. Please stop blaming yourself. Please.

—Please leave this place again, he says. Leave and never come back. Please.

It's early evening and I'm on my way home to have dinner with Kevin and Casey.

She's doing salad, green beans, and baked potatoes, and I'm grilling steaks.

It's been a beautiful day—bright, crisp, comfortable, but now, as the sun makes its final descent, the earlier coolness is returning.

Driving down Lake Grove Road, I realize just how happy I am and I realize just how much it has to do with my relationship with Reggie.

What a gift she is. What an unexpected gift.

Nearing the landing, I see that it is empty, not a single soul in sight, but I hear the harsh incessant honk of a car horn.

As I turn onto Byrd Parker Drive I see the source.

It's coming from a small, red, cheap faux sports car.

I pull into the yard behind Sylvia's old Chevy and jump out to see what's going on.

Approaching the car, I see Eric Layton, Becky's husband and Reggie's brother-in-law, laying on the horn.

When I tap on the window, he jumps, then looks up at me with a wounded, angry expression of embarrassment.

It takes him a minute but eventually he rolls down the window.

—What's going on? I say.

A Certain Retribution

—The fuck you doin'? he says. That's a good way to get your ass shot.

I laugh, finding the threat from this little man mama's boy as much amusing as annoying.

—Is something wrong? I ask. Why are you sitting out here honking your horn at the home of a very sick woman?

—I tol' Beck and Lex to be quick, he says.

—Oh, she's taking too long with her dying mother.

—Why're you here? he says. What's this got to do with you?

—Have you even been inside? I say.

—I avoid the old bitch as much as I can. She doesn't like me and I don't like her.

Just then the front door of the trailer bursts open and Becky and Lexi Lee rush out, stumbling down the steps, tripping over the oak roots in the yard as they do.

—Eric, honey, I'm so sorry, Becky says before she even reaches the car. I've been trying to get out of there, but Mom got choked and I had to help her.

—Where the hell is Reggie? he says. She's supposed to be looking after the . . . your mom. After all, she's living here rent free, right?

Lexi Lee is small and looks frail and may even be trembling as her mother helps stuff her into the car's nearly non-existent backseat.

—Merrick, Becky says to me across the roof of the car before she gets in, could you check on her? Maybe sit with her until Rain or Reggie get here?

Before Becky has her door shut, Eric is backing out of the yard, revving the small, airy-sounding engine as he does.

—I saw Allen Maddox today, Reggie says.

—I feel so bad for him, I say. Seems so lost.

We are alone in her living room, Rain and her mom long since asleep. The room is nearly dark, the only illumination

93

coming from above the sink in the kitchen and the nightlight in the bathroom down the hallway.

—I'm raw from it, she says. Opened up some old wounds inside me.

I start to say something but stop and just nod and listen.

Through the windows across the back, the riverbank on the opposite side can be seen intermittently in the flicker of distant heat lightening.

—He was such a sweet boy. Smart. Funny.

—What happened to him? I ask.

—He took me to my junior prom. It was such a nice night. We were friends. Good friends. He wanted more but I just never felt that way about him. He was like my brother, a role he seemed to embrace fully once I made it clear that's all I could ever see him as.

She pauses and I nod, though she's not looking at me.

—We had such a good time. No pressure. No drama. Just fun. We danced and ate and hung out with our friends. Even got voted king and queen. Throughout the night Robin and Donnie Ray and a few of their friends made some crude comments. They were always assholes. That night they were drunk assholes.

Her mom coughs from down the hall and she waits to see if there is more to come.

—A group of us went out to Iola afterwards. Built a fire. Played some music. Drank some beer. Hung out. Eventually Robin and Donnie Ray and them showed up. They were so belligerent, such dicks, that the party began to disband. I don't know why we didn't leave sooner. I guess I just didn't want to be run off from my own party by such fuckin' losers. By the time we gave in and started to leave we were about the only ones left. Robin and Donnie Ray started picking on us. Wouldn't let us leave. Kept challenging Allen. They tried real hard to get him to fight them but it was four against one.

—Who all was it?

—Robin, Donnie Ray, Skip, and Skeeter. They've always been his little posse. Hell, they still are. Only with badges now.

A creak in the hallway makes her stop again and listen,

but when there's nothing else she continues.
  —He handled it all extremely well. Kept his cool. Acted like it was all a big joke. Disarmed them in a lot of ways. Eventually they said if we'd just have one drink of their homemade hooch with them they'd let us go. So we did. When we woke up the next morning we had been roofied and raped.
  —Oh God, Reggie, I'm so sorry, I say.
  Now I know why she is so defensive, why she wears the emotional armor, why she's always armed.
  I wrap her up in my arms and hold her for a long moment.
  —Told you I had a history with the son of a bitch.
  —And seeing Allen . . .
  —I almost didn't recognize him. He's so . . .
  —Was he raped too?
  —Roofied. Not sure about raped but I always suspected. Something about the way his clothes were and the way he acted.
  —What happened next?
  —I got in trouble for staying out all night, blamed for what happened, my passive parents didn't want to rock any boats, acted like they really didn't believe me anyway. My whole world ended. I plummeted. Lost all sense of myself. Wasn't like I was the most secure person to begin with, not the most confident, but after . . . and the way they looked at me. Robin and the rest of them. They knew I knew and couldn't do anything about it and . . . it was hell. The only reason I started dating Rain's douchebag dad was that he stood up to them, even beat Donnie Ray's ass the year before. He was as big an asshole as them. I just didn't . . . If I had had anyone I could count on. . . If my parents would've been there for me, defended me, done anything at all . . . But it turns out as bad as I've had it, Allen's had it worse.
  —Not worse, I say.
  —I've survived. You should see him.
  —I have.
  —Anyway . . . wasn't planning on telling you that. But you already knew I was damaged goods. Now you know why. Cut your losses. Get out now.

I shake my head.

—I mean it. I don't want to go any further into this thing just to have it yanked out from underneath me.

—I'm not yanking anything. You're the only one who keeps trying to end it.

—Just because it's inevitable. Might as well do it now.

—No, I say.

—I'm not playing, Merrick. I can't do this. You're not just another loser. This is real. I don't do real.

I lean in and kiss her.

She tries to protest, talking into my lips and mouth, but I keep kissing her.

—What do you want from me? she asks.

—Just you. Just the way you are.

—You don't want me.

—I do.

—You don't. Or you won't soon enough.

—Come on, I say, standing, taking her hand and pulling her up with me.

—Where are we going?

—To bed together. We can sneak into your room here or we can go to my place, but we're going to make love and sleep in each other's arms.

—We can't. I can't.

—We can. We will.

—I'm not ready.

—Yes you are. I can tell. I know it. Trust me.

—I can't.

—You can. You should.

—Will you be here tomorrow?

—I will, I say. I promise.

We make love quietly but intensely and passionately in the small, paneled walls room, her teenage son on one side, her dying mother on the other.

A Certain Retribution

It is fun and healing and extremely satisfying, and about as good as a first time can be, and in the morning when she wakes, I am still here.

—You're here, she says.

—Told you I would be.

—You're sexy, she says. And a goddamn good lay. Wow.

—You're beautiful, so generous, so good.

—I thought the third time was our best, she says.

—I was partial to the second, but they were all good.

—That's the first first-time sex where I didn't have to get myself buzzed to even do it. And it was so . . . I mean, it wasn't all that awkward or anything.

—You are truly lovely, I say.

—You don't think I'm too thick, tits too small, ass too big?

—I think you are perfect. Truly perfect. Your body is amazing. I can't wait to spend more time with it as soon as possible. What are you doing tonight?

—Really?

—Really.

—I have patrol.

—Then before and after—and during if you get a coffee break.

She smiles and it's as radiant as the morning.

On my upper right arm and near the center of my left thigh I have small scars from where the creep who kidnapped Casey shot me when I was trying to get her back.

Reggie's finger finds the one on my arm and adjusts to examine it.

—What the fuck? she says in genuine surprise. That's from a gunshot.

—It is, I say. There's a matching one over here.

—What's the story and why didn't you lead with it? You could've gotten into my panties a lot, lot sooner.

I tell her.

She smiles in true delight.

—I bedded a badass.

—Hardly.

—You got her back, she says.
—I did.
—And the kidnapper?
—Won't ever kidnap anyone again.
—On account of him being in prison or the ground?
—Ground.
—See? Badass.
—Only did what any decent dad would do. I got lucky.
—Any remorse for taking a life? she asks.
—Not his. Not a second.
—Not saying you're not a gentle, kind man. You are. You're the most gentle, kind man I've ever known, but you're also a bit of a badass. Deal with it.

I laugh.

—And I love that you don't advertise it.
—What happened to Rain's back? I ask. I noticed burn scars the other night.
—Can we not talk about it right now?
—Of course. Sorry.
—Everything's so perfect and I don't want to think about how I could've ever been involved with an ignorant, evil loser like Tommy Ray Williams.

Tommy Ray Williams is the most corrupt county commissioner and Pentecostal preacher Gulf County has ever produced. And that's saying something. He's also the charming sociopath who seduced the insecure, inexperienced child version of Reggie into impregnation and an ill-fated attempt at domestication.

—His dad did that to him?
—Another time.
—Sure. Sorry.

We fall quiet a few moments. She continues to caress my scars.

—Merrick McKnight, she says. In my bed. Waking up beside me. God you're gorgeous.
—You're luminous, I say. I really do adore you.
—That's just infatuation or the sex talking, she says. It'll wear off.

A Certain Retribution

—Actually, it's not. I know infatuation. I've been infatuated before. But the only way to see who's right is to stick around.

—I shouldn't tell you this, she says. It breaks all of my rules to. But . . .

—Yeah?

—You could so use this info against me but somehow I don't think you will. Obviously I don't think you will or I wouldn't be telling you or thinking about telling you. Maybe I shouldn't. I shouldn't.

—Tell me now or I'll wake up your son and mother and tell them what we did last night.

—I don't know if you'll think this is sad and pathetic or a total exaggeration, but that was the best sex of my life. Our first night together you gave me the best sex of my entire life. I realize I haven't had all that much, but I've had enough to know what good is, and mister let me tell you that was some stinkin' good sex.

—Cowgirl, you ain't seen nothin' yet. Better put your boots in the stirrups and grab the horn and the reins and hold on, 'cause we're just gettin' started.

—God I love the sound of that. Makes me so wet when you call me cowgirl.

She giggles. It's soft and sweet and makes her sound like a giddy teenager.

—What is it? I ask.

—I'm not just bedding a badass, she says, but he's a badass in bed.

—What are these? I ask.

I have awakened again to find her sitting up in bed, an open file box in front of her, folders scattered around it.

—My files on every one of the fuckers, she says.

—Robin and the rest?

She hands one to me.

It looks like something a cop would create. Organized. Thorough. Official-looking, though it's not.

—These are evil people with a pattern of cruelty, brutality, and abuse, she says. And now it's part of their job description.

—Are they the reason you're here? Did you come to . . .

—I came for Mom, she says. But also to stop them.

I nod.

—Whatta ya think? she says.

—That they need stopping, I say. That you're the woman to do it and I'm the man to help.

I am with her later in the day when she gets the news.

In an attempt to reassure her, to make certain she knows our lovemaking last night signified the next level and not the end of our relationship, I arrive at her office with lunch from RD's, a small bouquet of cotton I drove up to a farm just past the county line to pick, and a F'real Mint Chip Milkshake.

—I'm too busy fighting crime to take a lunch, she says.

Her desk is mostly empty and I spread everything out in front of her.

—Hellfire, son, you get a little and you go crazy, don't you? How long's it been?

I begin bagging everything back up.

—I know what you're doin', she says.

—You do?

—It's obvious.

—Good.

—You're trying to make sure you get some more.

I keep bagging.

—I'm kidding, she says. It's the sweetest thing anyone's ever done for me. You're . . . this is just . . . You got the milkshake I love, my RD's cheeseburger the way I like it. How'd you know? You even made me a cotton bouquet—so much better than flowers. Thank you.

A Certain Retribution

—You're welcome. Let's eat.

—Hell man, you give me the best sex of my life on our first night together, I should be bringing you lunch and gifts and—

Her phone rings.

—Hold that thought, she says as she answers it.

—Hello . . . This is she.

For the next several minutes, as she listens and gives an occasional *uh huh*, her countenance falls and she stops eating, even eventually putting down her milkshake.

—And you're sure? she says. It's that conclusive? Couldn't be faked?

She listens.

—Okay, she says. No, I appreciate it. Thanks for—thank you.

After ending the call she drops her phone on the desk.

—What is it? I ask. What's wrong?

—Robin didn't kill Dahl.

—How can you know that?

—No one did. ME says it's a suicide. Angle of the projectile is consistent with a self-inflicted gunshot wound to the head. Gun powder residue on his hand.

—What about where the gun was found? I say.

—Consistent with the recoil of the weapon.

—I thought the angle of the entry wound was a little farther to the back than it should've been.

—Evidently not.

—What about the second round? I say. Two were fired, only one found.

—Fired at a different time. Maybe even a short while before he committed suicide. No way to know when or where exactly, just that it's unrelated to the act of taking his own life.

The next body is found a few nights later when we're at the final home football game of the season. Together. As a couple. On display.

It seems as though the entire town is at the game, as if there's no one left anywhere else to kill or be killed.

Actually, the game is against inner-county rival Port St. Joe, so it seems as though the entire county and not just the town is here.

The left side of the field is a sea of red and white, the right a sea of purple and white. On the field itself for both the gators and the sharks, boys who look too small to be playing high school football are engaged in a battle that seems nothing less than epic to them.

By the time we arrive, the bleachers are full and we, like so many, stand the entire time.

We're running a little later than we planned because the hospice nurse had a flat tire on her drive over from Panama City and was late arriving to take over care of Sylvia.

We're directly behind the goalpost in the end zone, the waist-high chain-link fence before us lined with watchers, men mostly, their animated interactions serving as the foreground for the frame of the game. All around us people are moving, walking past us both in front and behind—kids running, chasing, playing, teens walking, scanning, preening, young mothers holding the hands of small children, JV cheerleaders, their hair up in red-and-white pompom ponytails selling programs or raffle tickets, Wewahitchkans of every age headed to or from the concession stand, to or from the restroom.

Though Reggie recently received her uniform she is not wearing it tonight. Instead she has jeans and boots and a blue windbreaker that has WPD on it and nearly conceals the holstered weapon on her hip.

The night is crisp and cool, the ground beneath us damp, the sky above us clear and bright, a nearly full moon seeming to spotlight the planet.

The smell of hamburgers sizzling on the grill and the buttery aroma of freshly popped popcorn permeates the air around us so heavily it seems palpable, as if the simple act of breathing is nearly the equivalent of tasting.

Nearly everyone who walks by speaks or waves or

smiles, many stopping to ask when we started dating, a startling number unaware Reggie was even back in town or that Wewa once again had a police department.

Rain stops by with his new girlfriend, a bleach-blond pixie with heavily made up brown eyes, skinny jeans, and camo Converses. She is far more friendly than I expect—especially to Ms. Summers, who she clearly wishes to ingratiate herself with.

—He works fast, I say.

—He's always quick to get a girlfriend, she says. Just doesn't keep them long. Speaking of working fast, what about her? Was it just me or was she trying to get me to adopt her?

A little later, Casey and Kevin stop by on their way to the concession stand.

—Somebody's hungry and thirsty, Casey says.

—ME, Kevin shouts. Hey Merrick. Hey Merrick.

—Hey man. How are you? Enjoying the game?

Beginning to tower over his older sister, Kevin's large, soft pale body is pushing six feet tall. He has close-cropped sandy-blond hair and fingernails that perpetually need cutting.

—Hey Merrick. Merrick. Hey Merrick, did you know, did you know that the first famous Super Bowl commercial was in 1974? And was an ad for Noxzema, featuring NFL quarterback Joe Namath. Did you know that?

As he talks he repeats himself often, places emphasis on random words, rocks back and forth, and uses his hands a lot.

—I didn't, I say. Hey man, do you remember Reggie?

—Hey Kevin, she says. What's up man?

—Hey Merrick. Hey Merrick did you know that with almost one billion dollars in yearly revenues, the NFL is the world's richest professional sports league? Did you know that?

—I didn't.

Kevin doesn't care for football as a sport very much at all, though he does enjoy coming to the games, but has an encyclopedic knowledge of nearly any topic that comes up, including arcane trivia, facts, and figures not even the most avid fans are aware of.

—Hey. Hey. Hey Merrick. Did you know that there is no network footage of the first Super Bowl? Did you know that?

Hey. Hey Merrick. Guess what? Guess what? It was reportedly taped over for a soap opera.

—Wow, I say. I didn't know that.

—I did, he says.

—We probably won't stay too much longer, Casey says. It's a little too much stimulation.

—I'll be home to help soon, I say.

She shakes her head.

—Don't be a daft prick, dude, she says. We'll be fine. You and Reggie do something fun. If you're home before two I won't let you in.

I smile.

—Thanks Casey. Call if you need anything.

Eventually Don Baxley, the one city commissioner who voted against making Reggie police chief, walks up.

A thin man pushing hard against seventy, he's by far the oldest commissioner on the board. One of the few remaining commercial farmers in the area, he's been a widower for as long as I have known him. He has the appearance of a man who gives no thought to his appearance, faded work jeans tucked into weathered work boots, old, wrinkled button-down shirt, silver framed glasses with thick lenses held together by duct tape.

—Glad I ran into you, girl, he says. Been tryin' to catch you at your office but can never find you there.

—Then you're not tryin' very hard, I say, because she's almost always there.

He ignores me.

—I'm a straight shooter, he says to Reggie, and I'm told you was too. So tell me how all this come about?

—All what?

—Never felt so ambushed in all my life. And I fought in Vietnam. I go in there expecting to discuss the possibility of ending our contract with the sheriff's department and reinstating our own police force, and the next thing I know it's happening with you as chief.

—I wasn't even there, she says.

—Ain't talkin' about what happened there so much as

before we ever got there. I ain't mad at you. I just want to know how you got the job, what you had to do, who was involved. Citizens of our town have a right to know.
—I didn't do anything or anyone to get this job, if that's what you're implying. The only thing I did was apply.
—Who contacted you? he asks. Or who'd you contact?
—You need to talk to the other commissioners about all that, she says. I got nothin' to do with anything political or any infighting or posturing. All I know is I was hired to do a job and I'm doing it.
—Are you? Who's watching the town while you're here at the game?
—I left Barney in charge, she says.
—Who?
—Officer Fife. Very capable man.
—Don't know him, he says. It's like I don't know what's going on in my own town anymore.
—I'm sure that's not the case, she says.
He shakes his head.
—Governor was a good friend of your dad's, wasn't he?
She nods.
He smiles and nods as if that explains something.
—Governor doesn't appoint police chiefs, she says.
—No, but he does sheriffs. Some people're sayin' your true ambition is to be sheriff. If FDLE's little frame-up of Sheriff Wilson works and he has to step down, the governor will appoint an interim sheriff.
—Hey, I say, isn't Robin Wilson your nephew?
—Got nothin' to do with it, he says. I just want to know why this was done the way it was. That's all.
—Well, I'm sure you'll get to the bottom of it, she says. And when you do you'll see I had nothing to do with it.
After he is gone, I turn and consider her.
—Anything in what he says? I say. You want to be sheriff?
—Can't say the thought hasn't crossed my mind, but there's nothing to what he was sayin'. There's no plan in place, no conspiracy.

—What about your dad and the governor?
She nods.
—They were.
—Close?
—Very.
—He know you want to be sheriff?
—No. *I* don't even know for sure. Just said the thought had crossed my mind. And you're the only one that even knows that.

Before I can say anything, her phone rings.

Covering her other ear with her hand, she steps over to the fence around the field in an attempt to hear better.

With very little interest in the game, I watch the people instead of it, scanning the crowd, thinking about how I would write about it, what details I'd include, what I'd leave out.

I see Dad on the sideline with a camera taking pictures for the paper. The two guys he is standing with from the Panama City and Port St. Joe papers are only a fraction of his age, kids really, and it makes me feel bad for him.

—I've got to go, Reggie says, when she walks back over. Kenny Ardire found a body on the river. Thinks it's Donnie Ray Kemp.

We reach the landing at the end of the road to find Kenny Ardire and another man standing in front of Donnie Ray's deputy car.

The car is parked in the handicapped spot next to the two pavilions near the dock.

—Son of a bitch, Reggie says as we pull up.
—What is it?
—Things just got a lot more complicated.
—How's that?
—Lonnie Larimore, she says.
—Who?
—Dahl Roger's stepbrother.

A Certain Retribution

She stops the car and puts it in park a good twenty feet from where the two men are standing.

Leaving the car running, she steps out, standing behind the open door, and calls for Kenny.

I open my door and walk around the back of the car to her side.

—Kenny, come step over here a minute. Lonnie, you just go on and stay right where you are.

They do as they are told.

Kenny, a local property appraiser, is a tall, thin late-twenties man who stands at nearly six and a half feet.

—I need to know what's going on here, Reggie says to him when he walks up.

—I told you. We found a body in the water. We left it where it was. Didn't mess with anything. Came back here to wait for you.

—What're you doing on the river after dark? she asks.

—Broke down. Lonnie came and towed me in.

—So you weren't together until . . .

—He came and helped me.

—Where is the body?

—Downriver just a bit, he says. Right over there where the little river breaks off from the big at the foot of Cutoff Island. Caught in some exposed cypress roots on the banks.

—How'd you see it in the dark?

—Lonnie has a light mounted on his boat and a handheld. He was scanning the banks as we came in. His light hit it and he showed me.

—Okay. Thanks. Stay here while I go talk to Lonnie for a minute, then I'll have y'all take me to the body.

Leaving Kenny, we cross the parking lot to where Lonnie still stands at the back of Donnie Ray's car, which is still running.

As we reach it, Reggie steps past Lonnie and looks inside the car.

—We done looked in it, Reggie, Lonnie says. Nothin' inside. It's just running.

—You open the door, get in, touch anything inside? she

says.

　—No ma'am. Didn't even touch the handle.

She comes back from looking in the car to stand in front of Lonnie.

　—So tell me what happened.
　—We was comin' back from—
　—From the beginning.
　—Chelsey called me.
　—Who?
　—Chelsey Pettis. Well, Chelsey Ardire. Kenny's new wife. She called me and said Kenny went on the river to look at a piece of property this afternoon and it was getting dark and she was worried about him. They were supposed to go to the ballgame. He was supposed to be in before dark. She had been calling him but not gettin' an answer. She's worried. New bride and all. Anyway, I road down here. Saw his truck and trailer were still here so I put my boat in and went in search of him. Towed him back in.

　—When was this? she asks.
　—Which?
　—When did you arrive at the landing and put your boat in?
　—Not sure. Maybe seven somethin'.
　—Did you see Donnie Ray?
　—No.
　—Did he go with you to help you find Kenny?
　—No ma'am, he didn't.
　—Did you see anyone?

He shakes his head.

　—Nary a soul.
　—Was his car here? I ask. Up here running like this?

He shakes his head again.

　—Would've noticed, he says. Always got an eye out for five-o. Plus the shit was runnin', you know? No way I wouldn't've noticed it.

　—How long did it take to find Kenny and tow him back in?
　—Better'n an hour I say.

A Certain Retribution

—Who saw the body?

—I did. I was looking all around with my Q-Beam, scanning the trees and water and banks. Went right past it. Took it a minute to even register. Then I's like, goddang it, that was a man. I said, Hey Kenny look over there. That's a body. I let off the throttle and we slowed and turned around to get a better look. Sure enough it was a body. He's facedown in the water. Could tell he was a deputy from the uniform. Didn't know it was dumb dumb Donnie Ray until we eased him over. And that's all we did. Swear it.

—When you were puttin' your boat in and saw a running police car you didn't think it was strange?

—It wasn't here, Reggie, I swear it.

—I was sorry to hear about Dahl, she says.

—Huh? Oh, thank you.

—Were you gettin' back at Donnie Ray for that?

—For what?

—Nobody'd blame you. You can't just let someone take out your family like that. Got to do something. It's about justice. Retribution.

—I's told Dahl killed himself. Is that not right? Did someone—

—Even if he did, you know Donnie Ray and Robin and the rest of 'em drove him to it.

—Don't know any of the goddang kind, he says. And even if I did I wouldn't do anything about it. Dahl was one of 'em. Just like 'em. Every last goddang one of 'em's crooked as hell. But I didn't see Donnie Ray or his car. And I didn't do anything to him. And I wouldn't have even if I thought he had done somethin' to Dahl. But I didn't.

—Just looks awful suspicious, she says. You just happened to shine your light on him and point him out to Kenny. You were the last one at the landing. His car's here still running. It's all just a little too—

—Ask Kenny. Talk to Chelsey. Only thing I'm out here doin' is a good deed. Nothin' else. You's any kind of detective at all you'd know what everybody else already does.

—Oh yeah? What's that?

—Robin Wilson killed Donnie Ray to silence him before he rolled over on him.

Before we go with Kenny and Lonnie to find the body, Reggie pauses to make a few calls.

The first few are to the state's attorney's office, the county judge, and FDLE. The first two she petitions to let her handle the investigation with the help of FDLE and without the interference of Sheriff Wilson. Though she doesn't get a definitive answer in the affirmative, they both say they need time to think about it and talk it over, their responses are positive enough that she uses them when calling FDLE to say, among other things, given the investigation into the allegations against Sheriff Wilson she needs their support with the investigation into the suspicious death of one of his deputies.

Next she calls the medical examiner and notifies him of the situation.

Once the pressing business is out of the way, and both an ME investigator and an FDLE crime scene team are on the way, she calls the hospice nurse caring for her mom as she steps into Lonnie's old aluminum bateau boat.

—How is she? Reggie asks.

—I gave her a little something to help her sleep earlier. She's been sound asleep ever since.

—What was wrong?

—Just a little discomfort. Seemed slightly agitated. She's been resting comfortably ever since.

—I'm gonna be a little later than I thought, Reggie says. Rain will be there to relieve you on time.

—I might be able to stay later if you need me to.

—That'd be great. Let me know as soon as you know.

—I'll check right away and call you right back.

—Thank you. Did you hear anything earlier at the landing? Or on the river? Any kind of disturbance or . . . odd noise? Anything?

A Certain Retribution

—It's been all quiet on the river front, she says.

—Okay. Thanks. Let me know if you're able to stay.

She clicks off the call with the nurse and calls Rain while Lonnie eases the boat out into the wide river and begins heading downstream.

—Hey, it's me, she says. I'm very sorry but I've got a suspicious death and I'm gonna be later than I thought. I might need you to come home early and take care of Grandma until I can get back.

—But Mom—

—Sorry. The nurse might be able to stay, but if not I need you there. I'm sorry. I'll make it up to you and if you'll promise to really listen out for your grandmother, I'll even let your girlfriend come hang out with you.

—Thanks Mom.

—Just be home by eleven unless you hear differently from me.

—Yes ma'am. Will do.

We head down the dark river just a quarter of a mile or so to the spot where the Apalachicola and the Chipola separate at the start of Cutoff Island.

To our right the banks of the river are lined with fish camps, trailers up on tall stacks of cinderblocks mostly, including the one Reggie is now calling home, to our left, a thick black swamp and the houseboat with the eerie green glow.

The night is colder now, the biting wind chafing our faces, stinging and watering our eyes as we ride through it.

Even at the relatively slow pace we're traveling, we reach our destination inside two minutes.

The large moon is luminous looming above us, the well-lit night shadowed beneath it.

—Everybody pull out your phones, Reggie says. Lonnie, Kenny, take pictures. Snap several hundred. Get everything. The area. The body. Everything we do. Merrick, video. Same thing.

We see the body immediately, large mass of green uniform and wet hair bobbing in the wake of our boat.

—Shine your light all around the area for me, Reggie says. Slowly.

Lonnie does as he's instructed. We follow the beam along the bank.

The body is tangled in a nest of exposed cypress roots where previous higher water levels have eroded the sand and clay of the bank then receded again to leave the craggy wooden web uncovered.

—Put your light over here, Reggie says, pointing to the body. Actually, let me hold it. Merrick, can you and Kenny roll the body over?

We do, leaning over the side of the bateau, the boat dipping down with our weight and that of Donnie Ray.

Slowly, carefully, grabbing handfuls of shirt and pants, we begin to turn him.

I half expect him to jerk awake, flail in the water attempting to get away from us, or reach up and pull me in.

The water is cold, the body awkward, heavy, unhelpful.

Eyes eerily open, staring up at us. Wet, fatish face, puffy and pale, stringy strands of hair stuck to a large forehead. Sad. Pasty. Pathetic.

Small hole at the heart, watery blood still threading through the green deputy uniform shirt.

—Will you hold this? Reggie says, handing me the light.

We swap places and with the light and cameras trained on his chest. She unbuttons the buttons nearest the wound and examines it.

Small, single gunshot wound, just left of center.

Just then he begins to jerk and twitch and trouble the water around him.

Reggie jumps back as Lonnie screams.

—Oh my God he's alive, Kenny says, letting out a little high-pitched yelp of his own.

For a moment there is panic in the rocking boat, Lonnie and Kenny saying things I can't make out, Reggie falling back into me, me dropping the light.

—Grab the light, she yells. Be still everybody. Shine it over here. Here, help me.

I find the light, lift it up, falling toward the side of the bateau where she is.

A Certain Retribution

Both on our knees, we grab the side of the boat and look over into the hooded eyes and broad green-black scaly snout of a large American alligator.

The bottom of Donnie Ray's left leg is in his jaws and he's tugging at it, causing the body to appear to be twitching and jerking.

Reggie and I both snatch back from the side.

—Fuck me, Lonnie says when he sees the gator.

—He's gonna pull him down in the death roll, Kenny says.

—We've got to get him free, Reggie says.

—How? I say.

—Poke him in the eye, Kenny says.

—With what? I ask.

But before he can respond, Reggie is already hacking at the gator's right eye with the handle of a fishing net she grabbed from the bottom of the boat.

The gator lets go, disappearing beneath the dark water.

—Here, she says. Help me get him in. Hurry. Be careful. Watch for the gator.

Kenny and I help her, each of us grabbing the uniform so as not to put our hands any deeper in the water than we absolutely have to.

The entire time I am picturing a sudden lunging out of the water, a crunching down on my arm, a moment later my hand missing, my mangled mess of stub bleeding into the water, making the creature realize there is more meat to be had.

But we get the body into the boat without another sight of the animal and head back to the landing, shaken, jittery, traumatized.

—His gun is missing, Reggie says. Wonder if it happened in the water or—

We are back at the landing, looking at the body in the bottom of Lonnie's boat. Lonnie and Kenny are sitting under a park pavilion. We are awaiting the arrival of the ME investigator and the FDLE crime scene unit.

—May very well be the murder weapon, I say.

Her eyebrows shoot up.

—Could be, she says, nodding. I doubt it came out on its own. Everything else on his belt is still there.

—He arrives at the landing, hops out of his car, leaving it running, confronts someone, or goes to someone's aid—

—Or maybe meets someone he trusts, she says, like his boss and best buddy.

—And he grabs his gun and kills him with it.

—Loads him in his boat—or maybe takes him when he's still alive and kills him out there. We need to search the landing and where we found him for his gun, including dragging the river near those spots.

—Need to know from dispatch what he was doing down here, I say, but how can you?

Her face lights up.

—I could call and ask right now before they hear what's going on.

—You better hurry, I say. You know how word travels in this little town.

She makes the call.

While she does, I make one of my own.

—You guys home safe? I ask. All good?

—Sure are, Casey says. All settled in. How goes the date?

I laugh.

—What?

I tell her.

—Cool, she says. So you guys are just a little ways down from us. Need me to bring you anything? Coffee? Better jackets? Towels?

—Thank you, but we're fine. Casey, thank you for all you're doing for Kevin. Sorry I haven't been as much help lately. That will change soon. I promise.

When I finish my call, I step back over to where Reggie is now checking on her mom.

—The nurse is still there? How's Grandma? I never

heard back from the nurse on whether she was staying or not. Ask her to call me. If she's stayin' you can go for a little while. If not, I need you stay there and take care of Grandma. Okay? I'll be by as soon as I can.

Hearing her I realize again just how much pressure there is on her, how much stress she is under, and I wonder if I'm adding to it or helping take any off.

When she ends the call she looks at me and frowns.

—You okay? I say.

—Dispatcher said Donnie Ray is off duty. Shift ended at five. Last thing he did was patrol this end of the county.

—You guys get how serious this is, Reggie says to Kenny and Lonnie.

They nod.

—I need to know what you were really doing out here.

We have stepped over to the pavilion, still awaiting the arrival of FDLE and the ME, which we are told is imminent.

—I swear on the life of my new bride, I'm tellin' the truth, Kenny says. I was looking at a piece of property, taking pictures, doing an appraisal when my motor went out. It took longer than I thought it would and my phone was dead. Lonnie came and towed me in. We saw the body just where you saw it. I borrowed his phone and called you. We waited for you here at the landing. Didn't touch anything.

—Got no new bride's life to swear on, but everything I done told you is true. Am I glad the bent bastard is dead? You betcha. Did I kill him? No way. And I wouldn't have even if I had seen him. Ain't a killer. Hell, I pissed myself when the gator wiggled the body. But I didn't even see him. God's truth.

—Are there weapons in your trucks? Boats?

They both nod.

—Got a 12-gauge and a .22 in my truck, Lonnie says.

—12-gauge and .38 in mine.

—Y'all took 'em out of your boats and put them in your

vehicles before you called me, right?

—While we's waitin' for you to get here, Lonnie says.

Kenny nods.

—Not hiding anything, he says. Just . . . you know . . . gettin' 'em out of the way.

—FDLE is going to process your trucks and your boats, your clothes, your weapons. Everything. If there's anything you need to tell me, now is the time. Get out in front of this thing. Craft your story. I can help you. Nobody cares that this asshole is dead. In fact, everybody will be happy.

She turns to see the FDLE crime scene unit pulling into the landing.

—Last chance.

—I've told the truth and nothing but, Kenny says.

—Me too except for one thing, Lonnie says.

—Oh yeah? What's that.

—I saw the body on the way out to find Kenny. Saw who it was and pissed on it.

Later.
Colder.
FDLE is finishing up.
The ME investigator is long since gone.
Comforter's funeral home has come and removed the body, transporting it to the morgue in Panama City.

Kenny and Lonnie and their things have been processed.

They are standing before us in Reggie and Rain's faded old Wewa Gator sweatsuits, their's taken by FDLE to be processed in the lab.

—Thing is, Reggie says, if you saw Donnie Ray's body on the way out, then you saw his running car here before you left, and you've lied about several things.

Lonnie shakes his head.

—I swear on the life of Kenny's new wife I'm tellin' the truth. Everything happened just like I said.

—So you saw the car?

—No.

—Was Donnie Ray here when you got here?

—Listen to me, he says. The only thing I wasn't honest about at first was seeing his body on my way out to find Kenny, and that's it. I was embarrassed about what I done. It was stupid.

—So you saw his car sitting here running?

—No.

—You're tellin' me you didn't notice an empty parked police car still running?

—No. I'm not sayin' I didn't notice it. I'm sayin' it wasn't there.

—The body was already out there when you went by, but his car wasn't here at the landing.

—Exactly.

—The car's been wiped down, Sally Ann, an FDLE crime scene tech, is saying. Well, sort of. The outside and inside handles, the steering wheel, and gearshift. It's not a very good wipe down. Seems sloppy and . . . more of a quick smear. But it did the job. We got no usable prints on those areas.

She's a tall, athletically built blonde woman in her mid- to late-twenties with ice-blue eyes and something Nordic about her.

She's still wearing her bunny suit.

Reggie nods.

—So Kenny or Lonnie could've gone in the car or moved it or . . . anything.

—There's no way to know, Sally Ann says. The only thing we can know is that it's been wiped down.

—It could mean Lonnie is telling the truth, I say. Car was brought here after he left the landing and whoever did it wiped it down.

Kenny and Lonnie are in the Gaskin Park restrooms.

The other crime scene tech is in the van. Only the three of us stand in the vast asphalt parking lot at the end of the road.

Before us, the river meanders beneath the moonlight, its currents and ripples refracting and reflecting. Behind us, Lake Grove Road, empty, desolate, disappears around a bend a mile or so down in the darkness.

—Far as I can tell, the two men who discovered the body are clean, she says. Something may show up in the lab but nothing has here.

Reggie nods again.

—Best I can tell, Sally Ann continues, the victim was shot once at close range. ME investigator said there's an exit wound so we're probably not going to have the projectile for analysis unless it turns up where he was shot. There's no sign of it here—either at the landing or where the body was discovered.

—Any idea on time of death? Reggie asks.

—Just a guess. Based on the temp of the body, the air, and the water—and given the state of fixed lividity, etcetera, I'd say somewhere between seven and nine.

—We got the call at eight-thirty, Reggie says.

—That helps, Sally Ann says. So between seven and eight-thirty. And maybe even a little later. Seven-thirty even. That's about as close as we are likely to get it even after the autopsy. I think the body was discovered quite soon after death.

—Maybe that's because it wasn't discovered at all, Reggie says. Just staged.

—You really like Kenny and Lonnie for it, don't you? I ask.

She shrugs.

—Lonnie more so, she says. He or they set it all up then call me.

The two men emerge from the park restroom and begin walking back our way.

—One more thing, Reggie says. I thought dead bodies in water sank.

—In general they usually do, Sally Ann says. After a while, as gas builds up in the body it floats to the surface.

—That's something that takes quite a while, doesn't it?

A Certain Retribution

—Depends on the temperature of the water, etcetera, but usually a matter of days.

—So why was Donnie Ray floating? How was his body found so fast? Shouldn't it be at the bottom of the river? That's part of why I suspect Lonnie. He or he and Kenny kill him and place his body in the cypress roots and then act like they found him.

—That's certainly a scenario that makes sense, Sally Ann says as the two men rejoin us. We'll see what the lab can tell us.

—Can we go now? Lonnie asks.

—You could've gone a while back, Reggie says. We were wondering why y'all are hanging around. It's suspicious.

—I ever get a retarded notion to be a fuckin' helpful citizen again, Lonnie says, somebody please shoot me in my stupid head. I mean, goddang it. All we did was find a—

He stops as Robin's sheriff's car, lights flashing, speeds toward us and screeches to a halt just a few feet away, smoke and the smell of burning rubber rising from the asphalt.

Jumping out and slamming the door behind him, Robin, seething, storms toward us, fists clenched, jaw set, in attack mode.

—WHAT THE FUCK IS GOIN' ON HERE? he yells.

His eyes are wide and wild but locked on Reggie.

—I'VE GOT A MAN DOWN AND YOU DON'T EVEN CALL AND TELL ME? WHAT THE—

Kenny is closest to him and steps toward him, his hands up in a placating position.

With one punch Robin drops him.

Kenny hits the ground hard and doesn't move.

I step ever so slightly in front of Reggie, trying not to block her view or disrespect her in any way.

—WHO'S NEXT? Robin yells. I'M GONNA FUCKIN' BURY YOU ALL.

Reggie shoves me out of the way with her left forearm while bringing up her gun with her right.

—Think carefully about your next move, she says to Robin.

Without even a hint of hesitation he keeps coming,

raising his arms to attack her as he does.
She fires.
And once again what I think is a gun is really a Taser. And once again the darts find their mark and Robin seizes up and drops board-stiff to the ground, falling just a few feet from where Kenny still lies unconscious.

Girlfriend and hospice nurse long gone, we find Sylvia sleeping soundly in her bed, Rain just as out in the chair beside it.
—I'm so glad they're gettin' this time together, Reggie whispers.
I nod.
—Some people are just so much better as grandparents.
—Unfortunately. You need my help moving him to his bed?
—I was thinkin' we'd slip down to mine for a little while first.
Over these first few weeks of our relationship our lovemaking has been frequent, intense, incredible. Finding time and opportunity have been the only real challenges, but Reggie has looked for, found, and suggested those moments and small snatches of minutes here and there as much as I have. More.
We are well-suited as lovers, in drive, in desire, in every way. There's a quality and comfort to our sex and connection that convinces me its intensity and our insatiability has little or nothing to do with its newness or our relative unfamiliarity with one another, and I can see us being lifetime lovers, never growing tired or bored, never quite able to get enough of the other.
Before she comes, she places my hand over her mouth to help ensure we don't wake her son and mom or alert them to what we're engaged in just down the hall, and I love to hear her moan my name into my hand, love to hear her heightened breathing through her nose and feel the warmth of her breath

on my skin.

Very few women I've been with over the years came as the result of intercourse alone, and of those who did it was occasional, most of them most often requiring additional stimulation. Not Reggie. It's the most amazing thing I've ever witnessed in bed. She comes every time we make love, every time with me inside her, our entire bodies touching, pressing, feeling, experiencing the other's.

When we're finished—at least for the moment—and are lying beside one another, her, partially draped over me, we caress and whisper and revel.

—You always been able to do that? I ask.
—Do what?
—Come like that.
She shakes her head.
—I don't know exactly what you're asking, she says, but I haven't ever experienced anything like this.
—It just comes so naturally, easily, maybe even effortlessly. I figured it was the result of a lot of effort over the years, that I was the extraordinarily lucky recipient of some hard work on your part.
—Can't believe I'm tellin' you this, she says. Can't believe half the shit that comes out of my mouth when we're together. But I've not come a whole lot in my life. Hell, I haven't had a lot of sex since Rain was born—don't use that against me.
—I never would, I say.
—I know, she says. Or I wouldn't be tellin' you. Never been with anyone like you.
—Same here.
—Still can't believe I am.
—I still can't believe how much we have to fight to find time to be together and sneak around to have sex.
—It is ironic. Grown-ass adults.
We are quiet for a while, our breathing betraying our drowsiness.
—What kind of cancer does your mom have? I ask.
—Lymphoblastic leukemia. Bone marrow and blood cancer.

—How long does she have?

—The thing you learn more than anything else when dealing with something like this is that doctors don't know shit. Every estimate we've been given has been wrong. So I really have no idea, but I don't think it's very long. Hell, she could go into remission. I mean, it's an actual possibility. But it spread and she didn't respond well to treatment so . . .

—Do you mind that I asked?

—I love that you asked.

—Good, I say, because you're probably going to mind what I ask next. Are you using the time you have left to heal? To forgive her and accept her, to realize she's just a fucked-up human being like the rest of us?

She is quiet for a long moment.

—Some, she says. Not as much as I should be. Thanks for reminding me I need to be.

—You're not mad?

—Of course not.

—I don't see how you're doing all you're doing, I say, and doing it so damn well. And I can't believe you're able to fit me in the way you do.

—Yeah, it's too bad I'll have to drop you in order to spend more time holding hands and singing Kumbaya with my mom.

Reggie's phone rings as I'm getting dressed.

She frantically turns down the volume as she looks at the screen. Sitting up, her beautiful breasts bare as the sheet slides down to her waist, she takes the call.

—Reggie Summers.

She waits.

—No, it's okay. I wasn't asleep yet.

I stop buttoning my shirt and just stare at how lovely she is. Her mussed hair hangs loosely and gently frames the beauty of her face, its deep brown strands draping the smooth darkish skin of her shoulders. Her toplessness accentuates the upturned curve of her perfectly shaped breasts and the rich copper rose color of their asymmetrical areolas and erect nipples.

I find her unadorned beauty and unselfconscious vulnerability luminous and irresistible.

As she talks, I sit next to her on the edge of the bed. Taking one of her nipples in my mouth, I reach over and cup her other breast in my hand.

Her eyes widen and her expression conveys concern, disbelief, and delight, but she makes no move to stop me.

—Say that again, she says. I missed that last thing.

Her voice is different now. Slightly, subtly, undeniably.

—You're sure?

She waits.

—And why didn't you mention this before?

Another pause.

—Okay. Thanks for calling.

When she ends the call, she gives me a slap on the top of the head.

—I was handling official police business, she says. You can't just—

I look up at her.

—I can't not do that when you look like you look right now and have the girls out.

She smiles.

—That's sweet. You're forgiven.

—What was it?

—Huh?

—The official police business I distracted you from, I say. What was it?

—That was Lonnie. Says he just remembered something he thought might be important.

—Was it?

She shrugs.

—He probably just made it up. Says a man was over in Gaskin Park when he came to launch his boat to go find Kenny. Says he was so shaken up by everything he didn't think about it again until now.

—What was he doing?

—Says he barely noticed him. Wouldn't've thought about him again if Donnie Ray hadn't been killed. Says he was just hanging out, sittin' on one of the swings. Didn't get a very good look at him. Was a good ways away and didn't pay him much mind but there was something about him that was creepy.

—Creepy? Like what?

—Says he was disheveled. Kinda dirty maybe. Grown man hanging around a kids' playground. Thinks he may've been a vagrant. Says there were no vehicles in the lot.

—You think he just made it up? I ask.

—A vagrant did it is the oldest one in the book.

I laugh.

—There may be something in it, she adds. I'll check it out, but I think the most likely scenarios are Lonnie retaliating for Dahl or Robin covering his ass. And I hope it's the latter.

I nod.

—You know he's gonna retaliate, I say.

—Robin? Yeah. I hope he does. I'd love for him to really come for me. Love the chance to take him down.

—I know you would but . . .

—Don't think I can handle myself?

—I've seen you handle yourself. You do just fine. But you know he's not the type to fight fair.

—Neither am I.

I frown and give up.

—What if it's not one of them? I say. What if Lonnie is telling the truth? What if Donnie Ray's car wasn't there when he launched his boat? What if there was a man over in the park? What if Donnie Ray was already dead and he saw him just like he said he did, and his car was parked running at the landing when he and Kenny got back?

—Then I need to find the man in the park, she says, 'cause he's either a suspect or a witness.

A Certain Retribution

The next morning over breakfast, unbeknownst to each other, Reggie and I ask the members of our households the same question.

—You ever see anyone creepy hanging out over in Gaskin Park? she asks Rain.

He is hunched over a bowl of cereal, eyes squinting nearly closed against the early morning sunlight streaming in the windows across the back of the trailer.

—The hobo? he asks.

—The what?

—You know. The homeless dude.

—No I don't know. That's why I'm asking.

—He just hangs out there sometimes. Seems nice enough.

—You've talked to him?

—He's come down to the dock before when me and Hunter was there.

—Why didn't you tell me?

—Tell you what?

—What'd he say?

He shrugs.

—I don't know. Just the normal stuff. How're y'all? Catchin' anything?

—Did he ask you for anything? Say anything else?

—Like what? No. Nothin'.

—You see him again you let me know immediately. Understand? Don't go near him.

—Hunter said too bad there wasn't two of them. We could have a bum fight.

About five houses down and about three-quarters of a mile from the landing, I am sitting at the breakfast table with Casey and Kevin having the same conversation.

Casey has cooked a big breakfast—a not uncommon occurrence because Kevin likes to eat heartily at every meal, especially the first one.

Bacon. Eggs. Grits. Toast. All just the way Kevin likes it.

—Either of y'all ever see a man hanging out at Gaskin Park?

—Hey Merrick. Hey Merrick. Do you mean the hobo? Merrick. Are you talkin' about the hobo?

I look at Casey.

She nods.

—Lately there's been a guy over there some. Think he might be homeless. Not sure. He talked to us once when we were on our walk. Seemed harmless enough. Was nice to Kevin.

—He was coo-ool, Kevin says, bits of grits and eggs on his mouth. Hey Merrick. Hey Merrick. Know what would be cool? Know what would be cool? Living in the park. Wouldn't you like to live in the park Merrick?

—Y'all see him again let me know, I say. I need to talk to him. And don't go near him, just to be safe.

—I wanna have a sleepover at the park, Kevin is saying. Can I? Can I Merrick? Can I? Wouldn't that be coo-ool?

I'm on my way to interview a local beekeeper for a piece I'm writing about vanishing bees and the impact on the tupelo industry here and the ecosystem the world over, when I see Reggie standing at the landing looking out over the river.

I pull up behind her and get out.

—Morning beautiful, I say.

She nods and gives me a halfhearted smile.

It's still early and the morning sun has yet to burn off the chill in the air or dry up the dampness on the ground.

—You okay? I ask.

—Woke up to a call from a friend of mine who works in Judge Norton's office. Said Robin is taking out a restraining order on me and plans to arrest me and file assault charges.

I shake my head.

—Sorry.

—Judge is trying to talk him out of it, but . . .

—Maybe he'll be arrested before he can.

She shrugs.

—Anything else?

A Certain Retribution

—Just trying to figure out what the hell happened here. Honestly, I think I'm in over my head. I could not only fail at this but wind up in Robin's jail again. This time long enough for him to do real damage.

—Have you talked to FDLE or anyone about stepping in? The tech—what was her name? Sally something?—saw everything.

—I'll call 'em when I get to the office.

—Good. What can I do?

—Give me a hug, she says with a shiver. Warm me up.

I do, continuing to rub her arms as I release her.

—And help me figure this thing out.

—Okay.

—I'm really scared, she says. And I hate bein' scared.

I grab her and hug her again, holding her for a long moment.

She never fully gives herself over to it and eventually I let go.

—Okay, I say. What are the questions? Is Lonnie lying? If not, where was Donnie Ray's car when he first got here? Why would the killer have it at all? Why return it here and risk being seen after Donnie Ray's already dead down the river? Why didn't Donnie Ray sink? Did he go in the water here or somewhere else? If here, how was he floating?

—Everything you just said is predicated on Lonnie telling the truth.

—You think he's not?

—No way to know for sure, she says. That's why I'm lost. I just can't . . . I'm really starting to freak out.

—It's going to be okay, I say. I'm gonna help you. Hell, FDLE is on the case. We'll figure it out.

—I feel so weak and pathetic.

—Well you're not. You're the opposite. It's a feeling and it will pass. You're just tired and stretched thin and overwhelmed. Cut yourself some slack.

She twists her lips and nods, her eyes glistening.

—Thanks.

—A good way to find out for sure if Lonnie is lying

or not is a witness. My kids have seen the man he mentioned seeing when he first got here. If we find him—
—Rain did too. Called him a hobo.
I laugh.
—So did Kevin. If we find him maybe he can corroborate Lonnie's story. Or not. Either way would be helpful.
She nods.
And what about someone else who was here? Or saw what happened from one of the nearby camps.
—Planned on canvasing the area today. I just don't have the . . . I need help. I can't do what I need to do at the office if I'm going door to door here. Everything's gettin' so backed up.
—You want the door to door or the hobo? I ask.
—Huh?
—I'll start with the door to door while you go call FDLE and do what you need to do at the office. Then you can either come back and help or try to get a line on the hobo.
—You can't—
—Sure I can.
—What about your interview with the beekeeper?
—Can reschedule. No problem. Guy's my uncle. He'll understand.
—But I need to do the door to door. It's official police business. Plus it takes a certain . . . to get the info out of them.
—I've been a reporter my entire adult life. Longer. I know how to ask questions.
—Oh yeah? she says. You as good at answerin' them?
—Try me.
—How'd you get so sweet and I get so lucky?

Her office in the old city hall building is cold. And something about the temperature makes her realize how empty and austere it is.
The cypress plank walls are bare, as is the surface of her

desk with a few impersonal exceptions. A phone. A calendar. A beat-up old laptop.

Her environment has the appearance of temporality and unimportance, a transient quality that makes her question herself.

Do you devalue what you do? Do you expect to be booted out at any moment? Are you trying to protect yourself? Act like you don't care, won't care when they take it away from you?

Are you doing the same thing with Merrick? How long before you fuck up both? You know it's just a matter of when. It's what you do.

The phone on her desk rings and she is grateful for the interruption of her thoughts.

—Hold the line for Judge Norton, an unfriendly female voice says.

Here we go.

She braces herself, trying to think of how best to defend herself without coming across as defensive and to make her case without being too aggressive or argumentative.

—Chief Summers?

—Reggie. Please.

—Judge Norton. This is a courtesy call. I just wanted to let you know that at Sheriff Wilson's request I've spoken to the state's attorney and while we're not taking the case away from you we're not going to prevent the sheriff's department from investigating too.

—But—

—Not unless or until there are charges brought against the sheriff. It's not fair to prevent a man from doing his elected duty just because he's under investigation. You two can cooperate or run the investigations independent of one another. It's one of his own men. And he's the chief law enforcement officer of the county. Unless or until he is removed from that position I'm not going to tell him he can't investigate a case in his jurisdiction. Understand?

—Yep.

—Yep? Really? How would you like to be held in

contempt?

—I wouldn't.

—Then show some goddamn respect.

—Yes, Your Honor.

—You're not doing yourself any favors with that attitude. If you don't play well with others, you don't need to be in public service.

—Sorry. I'll do better.

—Now, he says, clearing his throat, Sheriff Wilson says you assaulted him when he tried to enter the crime scene.

—He's lying. He's the one who did the assaulting. All I did was stop him. He actually knocked a witness unconscious. There was no provocation. He's out of control, abusive, crooked. I have four witnesses that will confirm what I'm saying. Only one of which I'm sleeping with. And one that's an FDLE crime scene technician.

—You're sleeping with one of the witnesses in the case?

—No. To the assault. You want me to be respectful, then earn it. You want me to call you Your Honor, then act honorably. Stop protecting Robin Wilson. You're backing a losing horse. He's corrupt and crooked and is going down. And there's a very good chance he murdered the man whose murder you're lettin' him investigate. So—

The line goes dead.

—Your Honor? Your Honor?

Without cradling the receiver she punches in Maureen Evans's number.

—FDLE Executive Investigations Division. How may I direct your call?

—Special Agent Evans, please.

—Maureen Evans, she says, answering on the second ring.

—It's Reggie Summers from Wewa.

—Chief Summers. What can I do for you?

—You can arrest Robin Wilson. That's what.

—What's he done now?

She tells her.

—You think he killed Deputy Kemp?

A Certain Retribution

—I have no idea. Certainly have no evidence that would indicate that so far, but I'm just starting the investigation. He's being allowed to investigate too. You know what that's called? License to obstruct.

—I'm sorry I can't make this move any faster, she says. You know how these things are. It's a slow grind. We have to be thorough. An investigation like this can't be rushed.

—But—

—But, Maureen says, now this division will participate in the investigation of Kemp's murder too and it might be the very thing we need to make an arrest.

—Why's that? Your investigative division is already helping me with it. I want you concentrating on Wilson.

—Oh I will be, she says. Just two days ago Donnie Ray Kemp indicated he might be willing to cooperate for immunity.

—I seen the police car there, the middle-aged lady in housecoat and slippers is saying, but never did see a policeman.

I am standing on the small wooden stoop at the entrance to her trailer door, both of us looking at the landing as we talk.

Her small elevated trailer sits atop stacks of exposed cinder blocks and is nearest the landing—two places down from Reggie's and about seven from his.

—One minute the car wasn't there, she says. The next it was. I's cleanin' up. Our bridge club was here last night. Pickin' up. Straightenin' the place. Took some dishes to the sink. Glanced out my window. Landing is empty. Come back a few minutes later and the car is there but no cop.

—Did you see anyone?

She squints, purses her lips, and looks up, seeming to strain at remembering.

She shakes her head.

—Nope. Don't think so.

—It's very important. Did you see anybody at any time? Before the car was there? After?

As she repeats her earlier attempt to access memory, something glints over in the woods on the back side of Gaskin Park just beyond the swings.

Turning my head ever so slightly, I try to appear to be looking away from the park as I cut my eyes back and study the area where I saw the glint.

There's somebody there. A man. Dirty. Disheveled.

It's him.

—No. No one. Sorry.

—What about another vehicle? I ask. See any other vehicles before, during, or after the cop car was there?

She does her squinting, pursing, raising thing again, and again comes up with nothing.

I leave her my card, ask her to call if anything comes to her, and then walk toward the restrooms in Gaskin Park, trying to keep a covert eye on the man in the woods beyond as I do.

By the time I reach the restrooms, I can't be sure if he's still in the same spot or not.

Instead of entering the restroom, I circle around the right side, using the building for cover.

Standing at the edge of the small painted block building, I peek around the corner but see nothing. Either he's moved or I'm not looking in the same spot or—

A presence behind me. Movement.

Before I can turn to see who—

Blow to the back of the head. Blackness.

Later, when I regain consciousness, he is gone. I am alone in the park.

I feel for my pockets. Phone. Wallet. Keys. Nothing is missing.

Head throbbing, I look around, slowly searching a little way into the woods before giving up and going in search of pain reliever and Reggie.

—What happened to you? Dad asks.

A Certain Retribution

Unable to find Reggie or reach her on the phone, I stop by Dad's to do a little work on the *Breeze*. I've been neglecting deadlines and generally being an absentee son and partner.

—Lost a bum fight.

—Huh? You okay?

—I could use an aspirin.

—You got it, he says, already heading to retrieve it. But you're gonna need something stronger when you hear what I have to tell you.

—Then the aspirin can wait.

He turns around and comes back into the room.

—Some questions have been raised, he says. And I'm gettin' some pressure to—

—What kind of questions?

—About Reggie.

—What about her?

—Do you think she can handle a murder case?

—That's what people are already wondering? I ask.

—Not just that.

—I do, I say. I know she can. I also know she's not trying to do it on her own.

—I know you're helping her, son, but—

—I'm not talking about me. There's not a lot I can do. I'm talking about FDLE. They're assisting on every aspect of the investigation.

—Then we write that.

—Write?

—I think we have to address these questions as part of the coverage of the investigation, he says.

—We're responding to town talk now?

—It would give you a chance to defend Reggie. Let her tell her side. And it's not just town talk. There are serious allegations. We have to address them if we're to have journalistic integrity.

—Journalistic integrity? I say. Like not doing a story on Uncle Cornell's DUI when he was mayor?

—I should have.

—Or not giving equal coverage to those you differ from

politically?

—I always try to.

—Then you're not trying very hard.

—It's . . . I really have always tried to. I need you to point out every lapse in unbiased reporting you see.

—What serious allegations? I ask.

—I'm on your side, he says. But if there's something to it . . . you need to know and so do our readers.

—Know what?

—Do you have any idea how she got the job?

I shake my head.

—Why? What's being said?

—Doesn't matter. That it's being said does.

—None of it would be said if she were a man. What's being said?

—Nothing too bad, he says. Mostly that she called in a favor and that she's really not qualified. Could be as innocuous as helping her get home to take care of her mom. Everybody in the area owed her granddaddy something at one time or another.

—Four city commissioners ended the contract with the sheriff's department and hired Reggie to be police chief just so she could come home and take care of her dying mother?

—Did you know she used to date Phil? Some're sayin' she slept with him to get the job and stopped seeing him when she got here. Supposedly she was fired from being a DOC investigator and her last job was as a mall cop. I hear the *News Herald* and the *Star* are already working on stories about her. We need to do our own. Where are you going?

—You know how Donnie Ray was wearing that windbreaker? Sally Ann asks.

—Yeah? Reggie says, surprise in her voice.

The crime scene tech's question comes without preamble as soon as Reggie answers her phone.

A Certain Retribution

—That's a possible answer to why he floated, she says. If he floated.

—Huh? How?

—If it was zipped up and air got trapped in it, it might have provided just enough buoyancy to keep his corpse on or near the surface.

—Oh. Wow.

—Just one possibility, but if he was dead and went into the water upstream it might explain why he got caught in the cypress roots instead of sinking like you'd expect.

—Thanks Sally. I really appreciate it. That helps a lot.

—May have nothing to do with what really happened but wanted to throw it out there as a possibility. We'll know more after the autopsy.

As she cradles the receiver, she realizes someone is in the building.

Unbuttoning the top strap of her holster as she stands, she pauses a moment to listen before stepping around her desk, out of her office, and into the hall.

His back is to her, but she knows instantly who it is.

How can someone's posture be so idiosyncratic and identifying? How can it reveal so much about the man?

He turns slowly toward her.

Hips jutted out. Chest back. Head cocked to the right. Hands down near his junk. Arms bowed out as if too big, too muscular to hang normally, though they aren't.

—Need to talk to you, Regina.

And that sneer. That goddamn smug-ass, self-amused, alpha, below-average-intelligence sneer.

Tommy Ray Williams.

Slicked-back dark dyed hair. Too much product. Tight-fitting suit. Cheap, outdated dress shoes. Gaudy gold watch. Dull diamond pinky ring. Pale complexion. Light dusting of light brown freckles on skin with both a bit of fleshy pudginess and a slight melted burn victim look.

He has not aged well.

How could she have ever been attracted to him?

Insecure young girl. Traumatized. Vulnerable. Susceptible

to slick seduction. What an idiot.

No. What an inexperienced, insecure, and exposed child. Stop being so hard on her.

This last voice is Merrick's and it buoys her and makes her appreciate him—especially all he is and is not that this crooked, brutish, benighted mama's boy is and is not.

As corrupt a county commissioner as this small county has ever seen—and that's truly saying something. An uneducated, drug-addicted, blunt, brutal, bully. Pentecostal preacher. Predator. Prolific liar. Manipulative. Morally bankrupt. Soulless sociopath.

—This shit with Robin Wilson's gotta stop.
—It will. He'll be dead or in prison soon.
—Don't think so.
—Bet on it, she says.

He leers at her lasciviously, actually licking his lips.
—Damn girl, you still look good.
—You need to get the fuck out of here, she says.
—Don't talk like that, he says. What kind of woman talks like that? This is a public building. I'm a publicly elected official.

—Wouldn't be if there was countywide voting, she says. Wouldn't be if your little gerrymandered district didn't hold all your crooked family and criminal friends.

She shakes her head. The same thing is wrong with national and local politics. This clown and all he represents is a microcosm of Washington.

—And just how the hell did you get this job, huh? he says. Who'd you put some of that tight little pussy on? It is still tight, isn't it? It'd have to be to get your unqualified mall cop ass this job.

Her face must betray her pain and embarrassment. She can see him savoring the blood in the water.

—Oh yeah, I done my homework. I know all about you.
—Be the first time in your life you've done any, she says. And I promise you, you don't know shit about me.
—You forget who you're talkin' to. I know everything about you—what makes you cream your little panties, what

makes you buck wild like a damn donkey in heat. I know your secrets and your weaknesses and—

 Before she realizes what she's doing, she draws her gun and points it at him.

 —You've got five seconds to leave before I arrest you.

 —For what? he says, absently scratching his jawline with his too long thumbnail.

 —Sixteen years of back child support, you fuckin' backwards hillbilly deadbeat dad.

 He starts to say something but nothing comes out.

 —I know your constituents don't care because they're all members of your fuckin' criminal family, but do your parishioners know you've never taken care of your kid?

 —My what?

 —Your congregation, moron. Do y'all skip over the part in the good book that says a man who doesn't take care of his family is worse than an infidel?

 —They know in my youth I made a terrible mistake and married a unsubmissive faithless whore and that she took my son away from me so I couldn't be a daddy to him and raise him right. I take care of my family.

 —Five.

 —My real family.

 —Four.

 —Not some whore and her bastard child.

 —Three.

 —Your mama's sick because of your wickedness.

 —Two.

 —We're gonna run you outta town again you fat fuckin' dyke. You're an abomination.

 —One. Tommy Ray Williams you're under arrest for—

 —I'm goin'. I'm goin'. But only because I can't be around your adulterous ass one more second.

 He turns and swaggers out as if unaware his enraged ex-wife is pointing a gun at the back of his small head.

 On the steps out front he bumps into Merrick, but Merrick is the one to say excuse me.

 By the time Merrick pulls open the front door, she has

put away her gun but not her rage, not her embarrassment, not her livid, murderous malevolence.

—I came by earlier, I say, and I've been calling. Was that Rain's dad that just left?

I find her just inside the glass doors, face flushed, skin moist, eyes narrowed in anger.

—I can't always be at your beck and call, she says.

—What? I ask in surprise. Wasn't sayin' you should be. Are you okay? What's wrong?

—I'm in the middle of a fuckin' murder investigation.

Her tone is harsh and I'm a little stunned.

Rather than walking back to her office, we just stand awkwardly not far from the front door.

—Which I'm helpin' you with. It's why I was calling.

I try not to match her mood with my reactions but it's difficult not to become defensive, not to snap back at her, not to tell her she's got some real man-sized balls to be such a bitch to the only person trying to help her, the person who actually got knocked out for her.

—What happened to your head?

—The hobo knocked me out. What happened to your disposition?

—You know what? she says. I can't do this.

—What? What do you mean? Can't do what?

—This. Us. I don't know who I've been kidding. Myself, I guess. But I can't have a relationship right now. I just don't have time. You're distracting me from what I need to be doing.

—Seriously? You're really doing this?

—Sorry, she says, her voice softening a bit. I really am. I should've never got involved in the first place. I should've stopped it earlier. I just . . . I'm sorry.

—What did your ex say? What's really going on? Is it just your fear? Are you just freakin' out for the moment?

—No. My decision is final. I'm sorry. I just can't do it.

—You're just scared, I say. And overwhelmed right

now. It'll pass. I promise. Don't do this. We have something really rare. Don't toss it because of how you're feeling right this second. You'll regret it.

—Oh yeah? You threatening me? You gonna retaliate?

—What? No. What're you—that should show you just how off your thinking is right now. I would never threaten you, would never . . . Retaliate for what? I was saying you'll come to regret your decision. Sooner than you think. You know how incredible this is. We both do. It's . . . something like this only comes around once—and that's just for the really, truly lucky ones like us.

—Sorry. See? You're too good for me. I don't deserve you. Don't know how to be with a decent guy and the truth is right now I don't have time to be with any guy—good or bad. I don't want to talk about it anymore. Okay? We're done. That's it. I'm sorry. Have a good day.

I don't respond and we stand there in silence for a long moment.

—You need to go, she says eventually. I have so many things I need to do.

—Okay, but for your own good, so I can help you, I need to ask you a few questions first. What jobs did you have before this one?

—What? I've told you.

—I mean exactly what jobs. And did you have a lot of them?

—Rain was sick a lot and I was a single mom. I lost a few jobs over it. Why?

—What jobs did you work?

—I took anything I could, she says. I had to. I had no choice. I was a correctional officer. I was a DOC investigator. I did some private security stuff.

—I need you to be specific, I say. Was the private stuff a mall?

—I knew it, she says. I knew you would retaliate. I knew it.

—I'm tryin' to help you, to protect you. Tell me the truth. Was it at a mall?

—Among other places. Yes. Protect me from what?
—How did you get this job?
—You're just like all the rest. Get the fuck out of here. Now. And don't ever come back. I never want to see you again.

Collapsing into the chair behind her desk, Reggie wonders if she's just made the biggest mistake of her life, as tears begin cresting her eyelids and trickling down her cheeks.

Even if it's a mistake—and she's not copping to that—would it be the biggest?

If it weren't for Rain, Tommy Ray would've been the biggest mistake of her life.

With that stunted, self-centered sociopath disqualified from the running, what does losing Merrick—or the possibility of Merrick—have to compete with?

Prom.

Going to prom? Going with Allen Maddox? Could someone else have defended me better, fended off the monsters? Or going to Iola? Or not leaving Iola soon enough? Or not refusing to drink with Robin and Donnie Ray and the rest? So many mistakes. So many opportunities to prevent what happened. It wasn't inevitable. Wasn't fate. Was just a mistake on her part.

But is this? Is telling Merrick to fuck off?

It was never going to work and you know it. We're too different. Too— He's too good for me.

Hell, he's reporting on how incompetent you are. Not so sure he's all that good after all. You don't need a man. Never have. You're no good at relationships and all they do is muck up shit.

Yeah, 'cause my life is so good as it is. Wouldn't want to go muckin' up the perfection that is me.

Things get so complicated, especially with someone like Merrick. You actually fell for him. Nobody can fuck you up the way someone you really care about can. Dry your tears. Cowgirls don't cry. You're better off without him.

Not sure about that but I know for damn sure he's better off without me. I did him a favor. Saved him from the perfect storm that is me.

Thinking about prom and what happened and Allen forced her to confront something she knew she would have to eventually, but had put off for as long as she could.

Is Allen the homeless man the kids call a hobo and who attacked Merrick? Is he who Lonnie saw in Gaskin Park? Did he have something to do with Donnie Ray's death? Have to find him and find out.

—What happened with you and Reggie? Casey asks.

It's a few days later. I'm sitting in my recliner working on my laptop when she stumbles out of bed in the middle of the night.

—Why do you think something's happened? I ask.

She shoots me a look.

There's a sweetness to her sleepiness that breaks my heart, a purity and simple beauty and a vulnerability that spoke to the dad in me in ways I couldn't begin to understand fully.

—You're back to being here all the time, she says, and . . .

—And?

—I know you try not to let it show but you seem sort of sad again.

She's right. I am. I've tried to hide it from her, from everyone, but I'm no good at it. I'm sad. I'm lonely. Colors are muted. Food tastes bland. Music doesn't move me. I feel like I've been stabbed in the solar plexus, like I have a collapsed lung and can't breathe.

Unlike in my previous relationship with Regan, I don't feel desperate or strung out. I'm just sad. Just miss Reggie. What we had was so unexpected, so unusual and promising, that I can't help but mourn it, can't help but feel as though what could have been something truly amazing and singular was stillborn and will never reach fruition.

—Sorry, I say.

—Sorry? For what?

—For letting it show.

—You really haven't. I just know you. But you wouldn't have anything to apologize for if you had.

—Thanks, I say.

I always enjoy my late-night conversations with Casey, my heart lifting a little when I hear her sleepy feet padding down the hall. I realize now that part of the reason is that it's one of the few times we get to talk without Kevin, whose challenging communications, obsessions, non-sequiturs, and relentless repetitions make it difficult for us to do anything but respond to him.

It reminds me again of just how patient she is with him, how devoted and genuinely loving, and how I've never once seen her act put upon or play the role of martyr.

—So what happened? she asks.

—She's under a lot of pressure. Her mom dying. The new job. Murder investigation. And she wasn't sure she wanted a relationship when we started seeing each other. Was always having to talk herself into it. Think she's not had many good experiences when it comes to men.

—And so she tosses away a good one when she finds one.

—Something like that.

—So stupid. Why? Why are decent women attracted to not-nice men? What's wrong with us? For that matter what's wrong with you?

—Where do I begin?

—Seriously. There is a pattern, isn't there? Think about Regan.

—She was an anomaly.

—Hey I liked her. I'm not saying she was a bad person or even a bad choice for you, but she wasn't really available. And it seems like maybe Reggie's not either.

I shrug.

—You ever hear from her? she asks.

A Certain Retribution

—Who? Regan? No. You?

—Occasionally. I think she just stays in touch to check on you through me. But I never tell you because I don't want to encourage your pattern.

—There's no pattern, I say. Your mom was fully available and we had a very good thing.

—Maybe that's why you won't let yourself get involved with anyone who's really available now.

—Reggie is. Or can be.

—You sure?

—I am, I say, nodding. I'm not saying she will be with me. Just that she is capable. I know it.

—Well then what are you gonna do about it?

It's Tuesday night and I'm driving.

I like driving—especially at night.

I used to like driving even more—back when my new car was a retro deep water blue Dodge Challenger.

I bought it the week before I lost my job as a reporter and I enjoyed it as long as I could. Back when I was unemployed, untethered, unsure of much of anything, I'd wander around at night in that car. Lonely. Lost. Searching. Always searching.

When you live in the Florida Panhandle where empty highways connect the dots of small towns, racing down rural roads is a way of life. But it was more than that.

I had still been raw from the loss of my wife, my son—and with them the loss in a different way of Casey and Kevin. I had been trying to climb up out of the grief I was drowning in. Just going about it the wrong way.

Tonight I am in an old gray Ford F150 I bought from the St. Joe Company Timber Division after they had driven most but not all of the good out of it.

I missed my Challenger but nothing else about the time when I had it.

My plan is to wind up at Tucks for the dart tournament, but I'm riding around thinking and looking for Reggie before I do.

Talking to Casey, remembering my relationship with Regan, dislodged something deep inside me—something previously buried.

I had been so strung out on Regan, so addicted, so vulnerable to the intermittent reinforcement of her mercurial moods and inconstant affections.

What I had with Monica, Casey's mom, was so provincial comparatively. She had been so consistent, so unwaveringly steadfast.

Regan's availability, if not her desire, had been so capricious, so seemingly sporadic, and yet I didn't just walk away.

Before Regan—and after for that matter—I'd only ever do so much pursuing then I'd simply move on. I'd never before been willing to convince someone they should be with me. Prior to her I was gone at the first sign of ambivalence.

Why did I endure her vacillation so long? Probably because of the intensity of her interest.

Things with Reggie are so different. Or were.

There's all the desire with none of the desperation.

I'm more attracted to Reggie than I've ever been to anyone, our sex is already better than the longest relationships I've had, but there's something more mature, more comfortable, more positive than I've ever experienced in any relationship before—especially mine with Regan.

Why am I thinking about all this? Is it because something about the way I'm riding around looking for Reggie reminds me of my pursuit of Regan?

I've already driven by her mom's house and her office in the old city hall. Unable to find her at either place, I'm roaming the streets of Wewa on a dark, cold night with far more nights departed than remaining in this October as it eases toward Halloween.

I feel like a stalker.

And so decide to cut my drive short and head on out to Tucks.

A Certain Retribution

As I'm pulling into the dirt parking lot two things happen nearly simultaneously. I see Reggie's car—parked around back where it can't be seen from the highway—and I get a text from Regan.

I haven't heard from her in nearly a year.

Seeing her number vibrate its way onto my screen is disconcerting.

When I ended things with her I had blocked her number to remove all temptation. Since then I've had to go through the procedure to block it twice more as the previous blocks lapsed. Evidently it had elapsed again and I had failed to recognize it, let alone do anything about it.

Parking the truck on the side of the building, I stare down at the small screen of my phone.

I miss you—is all it says.

I've talked about and thought of Regan more today than any time since shortly after we broke up, and this is the day I hear from her. That's something I find difficult to dismiss as coincidence. I mean, maybe it is, but the odds are just mind-boggling.

Did I make it happen by talking and thinking about her? Did the energy of my attention attract her to me somehow? Did I talk and think about her so much because it was going to happen?

Do you miss me?—pops up on the screen.

Is she unaware of the block? Has she been texting all along? The texts don't sound like it. There's no frustration or anger or questioning why I'm not responding.

How often do I dream of someone then see them the next day? How often am I thinking of someone when they call or I run into them?

Are we connected in ways we can't comprehend? Do we dismiss as coincidence what we don't understand and can't explain?

Perhaps it is all random and chaotic and coincidental. Maybe the occasional seconds of synchronicity are the exception that proves the dissonance rule of the universe.

I stare at her texts long and hard trying to decide what to

do.

Was thinking of you today—I type. *How are you?*

And then I climb down out of the vehicle that doesn't feel like mine and go inside to find out my fate.

Reggie is sitting next to a man I don't recognize at the bar, eating a cheeseburger and drinking a Bud Light.

When she turns along with the other twenty or so people in the bar to see who is coming in the door, I nod and give her a small smile.

She doesn't respond.

Not far from her at the end of the bar is her brother-in-law Eric Layton. He sits alone, looking mostly down, hunched over a Platinum he keeps sucking on like a starving calf on its mama's hind tit.

The only other person who stands out at a glance is the corrupt county commissioner, Pentecostal preacher, and biggest mistake of Reggie's youth, Tommy Ray Williams. He's huddled up near the jukebox with a big-haired bottle-blonde who is not his wife, but keeps glaring at Reggie in the reflection of the mirror on the wall in front of him.

Stacy and Peach smile and speak to me from the other end of the bar and I walk over to them, grateful for the pleasant greeting.

—Want one of your little sissy boy drinks? Stacy asks.

—Pretty sure it was called something else, I say.

—Nope, Peach says, that's what they're called.

—That what y'all call anything that's not beer in here? I ask.

—No, Stacy says. We have respect for wine and hard lemonade, but for fuck sake you drink something named after a fruit and a girl.

—It takes a real manly man secure in himself and his sexuality to come into a place like this and say let me have an ice-cold Straw-Ber-Rita.

A Certain Retribution

—Don't know 'bout all that, Stacy says, but there's no judgment here.

—Yeah, I say, clearly little sissy boy drink carries no judgment at all.

Peach retrieves the drink and pours it up in a red Solo cup.

—Whatcha gonna do when a dude drinkin' a Straw-Ber-Rita beats you at darts? I ask.

—The likelihood is so minuscule, Stacy says, I've never wasted time even imagining it.

I smile.

—What happened to you and Reggie? Peach asks. Y'all are thick as thieves, then the next thing I know . . .

—She found out I drink Straw-Ber-Ritas, I say.

—That's all it'd take for me, Stacy says.

—Who's she with? I ask.

—Never seen 'im before, Peach says.

—Me neither, Stacy adds. Not much of a looker and he's way old.

—But, Peach says, he ain't drinkin' no sissy boy Rita, now is he?

—Thank you girls, I say. I knew coming here and seeing you was just the thing to cheer me up.

Later, I am sitting at the bar in the courtyard between Tiki and Tucks eating big Gulf shrimp with buffalo sauce and ranch when Reggie comes up to me.

—Hey, she says.

It's cold and I'm the only one out here except for the occasional smoker—of which there are none right now.

—Hey.

—How are you? she asks.

She's clearly buzzed. Not drunk. Not at all. Just that beer buzz that rounds off her rough edges and makes her friendlier and more comfortable with herself.

She shrugs.

—I been better, she says. You?

—Me too, I say.

—You really question whether I'm qualified? she asks.

—No, I say. I never have. Not even when you were. I've seen you work. I know how good you are.

—Then why the questions?

—To defend you. To write an article that answers the questions others are asking.

—Like who?

—I don't know. I was told the *News Herald* and the *Star* are doing stories. I wanted to get out in front of them with a piece that explains and—

—An unbiased piece?

—No, I say with a smile. Totally biased.

—That's sweet. You're sweet. Sorry I got so . . . for what I . . . for how I acted.

—Thank you.

—It was just the worst possible moment.

—I know how much pressure you're under. How's your mom?

—May be my imagination but she seems a little better.

My phone vibrates on the bar beside my plate and I glance at it.

—Who's Regan? she asks. Sorry. I shouldn't have even looked. None of my business.

—I wish it was again.

—What?

—Your business. Who're you here with?

She shakes her head.

—No one. Why?

—Who were you eating at the bar with when I got here?

—None of your business, she says with a smile. Who is Regan?

—Old friend, I say. Haven't heard from her in a long time. Started texting me out of nowhere tonight.

—Old friend or old girlfriend?

I shrug.

A Certain Retribution

—Actually, not sure she's either. Who's the old dude?
—My uncle.
—An uncle uncle or a come-sit-on-my-lap friend-of-the-family uncle?
—Ew-eww. Don't have any of those, perv. He's my mom's brother. Came to see her before she dies.
—Good, I say.
—Really?
—Not about your mom. Just about you not sitting on his lap.
—I've missed you, she says.
—I've—
My phone vibrates again.
—What's her deal? Reggie asks. She want you back?
—Do you?
My phone vibrates again and she picks it up.
—I'll take care of this bitch, she says. What does she mean she's not dancing anymore?
—She used to dance.
She drops my phone on the bar top as if something about it is suddenly repulsive.
—No way. Tell me you didn't date a fuckin' stripper.
All my old guilt associated with Regan comes roaring up from somewhere inside me.
—Are you—
—A filthy fuckin' stripper? Really? That's something I'd never have believed out of you.
I feel such shame in connection with Regan—shame that has little or nothing to do with her having been a stripper and everything to do with how I handled the relationship. I was so lost at the time, so untethered—so much more so than I realized. I was so weak and vulnerable, so lost and lonely. And it wasn't just the death of Monica and Tyler but that of my mom a couple of months before them. I had been unhinged, unmoored, unable to call upon any previous stabilizing forces—no bearings, no rails, no anchors.
—I mean, Merrick, she says. Really?
—That's my question, I say. Really? Are you serious?

—Strippers are drug addicted whores.

—All of them? I ask. Really?

—It's a deal breaker for me, she says. And you probably think it has something to do with how I feel about my body but it doesn't. Do you have any idea how many times Tommy Ray cheated on me with a fuckin' filthy stripper?

—I hope only once, I say. And I hope you're not so wounded over what happened to you that you would think every woman who has ever danced is a drug addict or a prostitute. And I hope you wouldn't write me off because I was involved with someone who danced for a short period of time.

—Hope all you want, but I can't—

—Casey danced for a while, I say. She's never done a drug in her entire life. There's not a whoreish bone in her body. Hell, she's barely even had sex at all—too busy taking care of her autistic brother.

—Glad we found out now, she says as she turns to walk back inside.

I shake my head.

—I knew you were wounded and a little defensive, I say. I knew you had been through some shit and that it had hardened you some. But I had no idea you were so harsh and hateful and judgmental.

—Well, now you know. And I know you fuck filthy whores.

—No, that's the irony, I say as she steps through the door and slams it. I never had sex with her.

—You live with death, don't you? Sylvia says.

They are the first words she says to me when she opens her eyes, as if they are part of a dream she is waking from.

I nod.

—Yes ma'am. I guess I do.

Seeing the light on in her room as I was on my way home, I've stopped in to check on her. Finding her sleeping, I sit for a while, watching, waiting, wanting Reggie to arrive home while I'm still here so we might talk some more.

—Your mom, she is saying, then your wife and son.

I nod, memories of them filling my mind.

The dim house has a quiet late-night quality about it befitting a conversation about death between a dying adult and one that too soon would be.

—Taken suddenly, she says. Without warning. Quicker than the time it takes to say it. Here one moment. Gone the next.

I try to imagine how old Ty would be now, where he would be in his development, what toys would he play with, what books he would've read, what he'd be into. I think how different my life would be, how different I would be as the father of a five-year-old.

—Guess that's how it happens with most people, she says. But some of us . . .

She stops, seeming out of breath, and licks her lips.

—Sorry, she says. Could I have some water?

—Sure.

There's a small beige plastic hospital pitcher and cup on her bedside table. I refill the cup with the pitcher, the icy water sloshing around inside it, then bend the flexible straw down to the right angle, and hold the cup with one hand and the straw with the other while she sips through it, her pale, dry lips less than an inch from my fingers.

—Thank you. There should be some lip balm over there somewhere. Could you hand me some of that too?

I do.

She shakily scoops a small amount of the greasy yellow substance onto the tip of her index finger and rubs it mostly on her lips.

—That enough? I ask.

She nods and I return the small cylinder to the table with all the other meds and caregiver accouterments.

—Some of us see death coming, she is saying before I'm seated again, like a car wreck in slow motion, hear it like a phone ringing in the middle of the night. In my case I get a little more time. Mine's like a slow approaching storm on the horizon that when it arrives will swallow up everything I have and am and then I'll be no more.

I nod.

Her hushed words are hypnotic, each rising out of her weak, hoarse larynx up through her dry mouth as if nothing is more important in this moment than saying them, and I try to take in every one.

—We don't get a choice but if we did, which way would you want to die?

I think about it.

—Without warning? she says. With a little warning?

—Like you, I say. I'd want some warning.

She nods her approval.

—Well, guess what, son? You get some. We all do. From that moment of lost innocence in childhood when we're first confronted with death, we're warned the dark horse is also coming for us. All I've been given is a vivid reminder and a compressed timetable.

I think of the profundity of what she's saying and it makes me want to weep.

—I've been given some extra time to prepare, to do what I can to make amends, to beg pardon, and I'm trying to use every second of it, but what if I'd've started when I was your age? Or Reggie's? Or even Rain's? Think about where I'd be.

Instead I think of where I'd be in my life if I had started earlier.

—Did you start when Monica and Ty died?

I shake my head.

—Not like I should have.

—Well, you've done something. I can tell.

—Not enough.

We are quiet a moment.

—Thank you, I say.

—I'm not preaching at you, Merrick. I'm really not. Hell, you seem to do be doing better than most. There's a sense of something about you, an awareness of death, a respect for life. I don't know for sure. Any more than I know why you're the one

A Certain Retribution

I'm tellin' all this to. Because you're here. Because you'll listen. I don't know. I do know that I'm past the point of holding my tongue. Way past the point.

—I'm glad for that, I say.

We fall silent a moment, and a moment later she's asleep again.

—Are we really living? I ask.

—It's too late for those kinds of questions, Merrick.

I find Casey on the couch, the TV on in front of her, though she is mostly dozing. Her face and eyes are red, her hair mussed and sticking up in the back. She is so sweet and sleepy and vulnerable it makes me happy and sad at the same time.

—Sorry, I say.

She hits a button on the remote and turns off the small TV.

The TV, like the rest of the things in the house and the house itself, are old and well-worn and in some cases antiquated. None of us seem to mind much—or even think about it until we have company or Kevin in his unfiltered bluntness reminds us. We are together. We are healthy. We have everything that matters.

—What do you even mean, are we really living? Do you think we're dead and don't know it? Did we all die in that car crash and . . .

—I meant are we . . . I don't know what I meant. Sorry.

It's amazing how much she looks like Monica used to look when she first woke up, and I find it disconcerting.

—No. What did you mean? I'm sorry. I just woke up a little edgy. Sorry. Tell me.

—I just came from talking with Sylvia, I say. She reminded me that we're all terminally ill, that we'll all be dead before we know it, and I just wondered if we're really living like that's true.

—I've always thought Kevin was the best at living in

the moment, in staying present, and getting the most out of everything he can.

I nod and smile.

She's right.

—Though you're not too shabby at it yourself, she says.

I smile at her and squeeze her hand and we are quiet a moment.

—I heard from Regan tonight, I say.

—Really?

—Reggie saw the texts and ended things between us.

—What? Why? You're not even considering going back to Regan, are you?

—Why didn't you tell me she was single? I ask.

—'Cause I didn't want you to even consider going back to her.

—Come on, I say. I'm exhausted. Let's hit the hay.

—Not until you tell me you're not even considering going back to Regan.

—I'm really worried about Reggie, Sylvia is saying.

It's the next morning and I'm standing at the end of Sylvia's bed after she called and asked if I could come over as soon as possible.

I am tired, having had a long, late-night conversation with Regan. The call went on as long as it did partly because of our conflicting agendas. I was seeking closure and a better, less-abrupt ending than before. She wanted to assure me she really was single and interested in seeing me again.

—It's not like her not to be where she's supposed to be, not to call, Sylvia is saying. She always calls to let me know if she's gonna be late. Even when she patrols all night she's always here before Rain leaves for school. Is everything okay between you two? When's the last time you saw her?

—Last night at Tucks. She was having dinner with your brother. I left before she did. Have you talked to him?

A Certain Retribution

—Yeah. He's back in Perry. Said he left before she was ready to last night. Is everything okay between you two?

I shake my head.

—I noticed she's been around more lately and not as hit-in-the-head happy.

—It was her decision, I say.

—She's been through so much. She really has. She got out of here. Saved her son. Saved herself I guess. But she's paid a high price for it.

I nod.

—I know.

—I don't think you do. You probably know some. Part of it is my fault. Mine and her dad's. We just . . . it was a different time. We were different people. When I think of all the ways I've failed that girl . . .

We sit in silence with that a moment.

—Of course she's gonna push a good guy like you away. Don't let her. She's testing you, seeing if she can. Doesn't even realize she's doing it. She's so scared of being left, of being betrayed, of not being protected. If she can push you away then you fail her test and she was right not to trust you. It's all subconscious, but . . .

I nod as I think about what she's said.

—I hope you'll reconsider letting her walk away so easily, she says. She really is worth the effort. I can promise you that. But whether you do or not will you help me find her? I can't. I'm so . . . useless. And I can't involve the sheriff. I don't know who else to call.

—I'm glad you called me, I say. I'll find her.

I find her car still parked behind Tucks in the same spot it had been the night before. It's empty and there's no sign of violence.

It's the only car in the lot.

As I'm pulling out my phone to call Peach, she pulls into

the parking lot, the big knobby tires of her long black truck splashing mud water out of the potholes.

—Hey ol' buddy. You lose something?

—Yeah. Reggie. Any idea where she is?

She shakes her head.

—Seems like she was drinking a lot last night. Sure she didn't just decide not to drive?

—Maybe, but she never made it home and she hasn't checked in and her mom is worried. Any idea who she left with?

—Give me just a second and I'll find out, she says. You mind pulling up a little for me? Got a food truck coming to make a delivery.

—Sure, I say. Sorry.

I jump into my truck and back to the far side of the lot out of the way.

When I return, Peach is punching numbers into her phone.

A few moments later a refrigerated food truck arrives, its air breaks blasting loudly as it comes to a stop.

—Let me take care of this, then I'll make some more calls, she says.

—Need any help?

She shakes her head.

—Thanks, but it's a small delivery and they'll unload it.

She unlocks the gate and opens the back door of the kitchen as a muscular man in his mid-twenties stacks boxes on a handcart, which he then rolls across the cold damp dirt of the parking lot, through the gate, and over to the kitchen door.

After stowing the boxes of food and supplies and signing the paperwork, she is saying goodbye to the delivery man as she gets back on her phone.

—Hey, she says. Any idea who Reggie left with last night?

She waits.

So do I.

—Was she here? How the hell'd I miss that?

When she ends the call, she slips her phone into her jeans pocket.

A Certain Retribution

—Stace didn't see who she left with but said she was drinking with Paulette Piercy.

Paulette Piercy is a habitually single party girl always up for kicking back and cuttin' loose.

Beneath her short, jagged jet-black hair, her overly made-up face shows smoker's lines forming around her mouth and eyes and in odd places on her cheeks.

I find her nursing a hangover on her shift behind the counter of the Dixie Dandy, a grocery store with a deli and gas pumps on Highway 22.

She looks like she didn't sleep at all last night and might possibly be wearing what she wore yesterday.

She shakes her head at me when she glances up from punching in lottery numbers into the large green machine.

—You seen Reggie? I ask.

—Oh no. Leave me out of it. I'll drink with you and even listen to your problems, but I ain't no marriage counselor and I ain't gettin' in the middle of no lovers' spat.

—Her mom's worried. She didn't come home last night. Hasn't called. Do you know where she is?

Her eyes widen.

—Meet me out front in five. It's time for a cigarette anyway.

Less than five minutes later we are standing at the corner of the old building, her puffing away, me trying not to breathe it.

—We didn't really start drinkin' until you left, she says. I don't know what you said to her, but whatever it was she was drinkin' to forget it.

—What did she say?

—I don't remember or she didn't say much.

—What do you remember?

She looks up as she narrows her eyes and furrows her brow in seeming concentration, taking the opportunity to get in as many long draws as she can.

—I can't remember much of anything from last night.

She smells like a gin-soaked ashtray and sounds like she swallowed sandpaper.

—Who'd Reggie leave with?

—No idea. I left before she did. I remember that. I mean we were both headed out at the same time, were both in the parking lot sort of at our cars, but I left first.

—You sure?

She nods and takes another long draw.

—Who was with her?

—No one.

—Anyone around? Anyone else in the parking lot at all?

—Not that I saw. We closed down the place. Don't think anyone was left. No cars but ours out back. I'm sure of that.

—Where do you think she is?

—I really don't know anything about her. We just hung out a little last night. Tried to drink a few troubles away.

—She didn't say anything that might lead us to her? Anything at all?

—We just sang with the jukebox and drank and talked smack about bastards like yourself. There were no deep and meaningful conversations.

—Think about it, I say. Who else was around y'all for any length of time at all?

—No one, man. Not that I can remember.

I spend most of the rest of the morning and midday working through a list of people at the bar last night given to me by Peach and Stacy. Everyone on it remembers the same things. Reggie was there with an older man. The man left. Reggie stayed. Reggie drank a lot. Reggie and Paulette sang with the jukebox and danced and had a big time and were still going strong when each of the others left.

And with every second and minute and hour that

ticked by I grew increasingly alarmed, increasingly convinced something very bad had happened to her.

In the early afternoon I call FDLE to report Reggie missing and explain the situation with the sheriff of the county, and am transferred Maureen Evans.

—Do you have any reason to believe he has her? she asks.

—His threats and harassment and penchants for retaliation.

—But no evidence or direct knowledge?

—No. Does that mean you won't look into it?

—Not at all. Just determines how we proceed.

By mid-afternoon I can think of nothing better to do than going to talk to Robin Wilson. So I do.

I find him at the St. Joe Marina.

He has just gotten out of a gathering—the Jaycees or Rotary Club or the Gulf County Republican Party—I'm not sure which, which probably doesn't matter anyway since each group consists of the same members.

We step down on the wooden dock for privacy and walk among the boats as we talk.

The day is bright and the sun reflects off every shiny, shimmering surface, but it is cold and the wind whipping off the water bites and stings and brings tears to my eyes.

—Thought I told you not to leave Wewa, he says.

—Do you have her? I ask.

—Who?

—Reggie. Is she in your jail again?

—My jail? No. Why?

—She's missing.

He stops walking and looks at me, laughing.

—Wait. You're tellin' me the chief of police in Wewa can't even find herself?

—Do you have her anywhere?

He shakes his head and starts walking again.

—Merrick, listen to yourself. What do you mean, do I have her anywhere?

—Do you know where she is? Have you seen her? Are

you getting back at her?

He stops walking again.

—I'm conducting a thorough investigation into Deputy Kemp's death, he says.

—That's Reggie's case.

—Actually, the judge ruled we could both run separate and independent investigations. Do you know who my prime suspect is for Donnie Ray's death? Reggie. She's crazy, man. She's come back here seeking revenge for something she made up in the first place. She probably ran. I'm coming for her—but not until I finish my investigation and have such overwhelming evidence the judge grants a warrant for her arrest.

We've nearly reached the end of the dock. This time when he starts walking again it's back toward land.

—When Donnie Ray was being murdered—most likely by you or one of your men in a futile attempt to cover your other crimes—Reggie was with me and the entire rest of the county at the Wewa-St. Joe football game. Hell, Judge Norton was there with us. Nobody's gonna buy any trumped-up charges you come up with.

He shakes his head and frowns as if what he's hearing makes him sad more than anything else.

—Reggie Summers is a crazy, fucked-up cunt. Always has been. You should hear some of the shit she did while she was away. She should've never come back here. Now I know she's got you wrapped around her little dick, but do yourself a favor and get the fuck away from her, 'cause I'm taking her down hard.

This time I stop walking.

Turning, I take a step toward him, rage filling my body, etching the edges of my words.

—Robin, I realize your days are numbered. The only one being come for is you. FDLE's net is closing in around you even as we speak. But if you hurt Reggie in any way, if you do anything to her, I swear to God there'll be nothin' left of you for FDLE to do anything with.

—Well hell-o handsome, Harvey Harrison says.
—How's Wewa's gay population? I say.
He smiles.
—Horny as hell, baby. Best not come too close.

Harvey Harrison, a large, muscular man with coarse, closely cropped early gray hair and beard, dark eyes and complexion, is one of the strongest, toughest, most entertaining people I know. He's also one of the most faithful friends. A few years ahead of me in high school, he was a cheerleader and both the prom and homecoming queens and the son of a Pentecostal preacher who tried to beat the gay out of him.

His voice is a low, gravely, soft guttural mess like that of an ancient aunt who smoked three packs a day for her entire life.

He tends bar and performs in the drag show at the Fiesta in Panama City a couple of nights a week and on the weekends, but he still lives in Wewa in the church his dad unintentionally left to him when he died suddenly and prematurely.

Though the mobile home he grew up in is still next to the church on Bay Ave., Harvey kicked out the congregation and converted the church building into a home as soon as he inherited the property.

Many of the congregants still refer to it as the abomination on Bay.

It's on the front porch of his church house that I find him, smoking a cigar and drinking Jack from the bottle.

He's wearing an enormous white T-shirt with a pale blue print of Muhammad Ali on it, mouth open, clowning, and the words Greatest of all Time, long pale blue athletic shorts that perfectly match the print on the shirt, and white kicks with highlights and logos of the same pale blue.

—You still blowing Chuck King? I ask.

Right down to business, huh? I like it. Yes, as a matter of fact, I am. His wife and Sunday school class still think he's straight as John Wayne, but he falls apart if I don't suck his dick at least twice a week.

—Good, I say. We need him for our plan.

—Our plan? he asks. Oh sweet baby Jesus Christ on a cross, please tell Daddy you're talking about a threesome.

—Close, I say. We need him to check the jail for Reggie Summers and keep an eye on the sheriff while you and I break into the sheriff's house.

Without hesitation he begins texting Chuck King, the deputy and Baptist deacon, who he's been blowing since the storied WHS senior trip of '84—the one that forever altered senior trips for the rest of us.

Harvey's lack of hesitation has less to do with his history with and hatred of Robin Wilson than it does our history, his unwavering loyalty, and his unending desire for the entertaining and thrilling, his insatiability for experiences that don't, as he puts it, bore the balls off him.

—Think he'll do it?

—Oh he'll do it—and if you'd ever let me suck your dick you'd know why. They don't call me goat for nothing', sugar.

—Goat?

—Greatest Of All Time. Wanna tell me what's goin' on?

I do.

By the time I finish, he's heard back from Chuck.

—He's on it. We're GTG, baby. Says the girl is not in the jail and the prick is in his office.

Robin's house is in Whispering Pines, a small subdivision just past the TL James ballpark. It's an older house, one of the first to be built back here in the mid- to late-seventies, and it's in disrepair—faded and falling apart, the yard unkempt and overgrown. Not to an extreme, nothing the neighbors would complain about, but obviously neglected.

We drive through the neighborhood and take a look around, figuring out our approach.

—We know he's corrupt as fuck, Harvey says.

—Yeah?

—Most people like that are paranoid as hell.
—You thinkin' alarm? I ask.
—Dog. Something.
—Be interesting to see, I say. I bet he feels too powerful. Untouchable. Invincible.

We complete our second pass through the subdivision and pull out.

—Was thinkin' we'd park over near the ball field, I say, and come up through the woods into his backyard. Cool with you?

—A big ol' bear like me. Baby I love the woods.

We park and he pulls out his small B and E kit.

We traipse through the pinewood forest, the undergrowth scraping his huge legs exposed beneath his shorts seeming to have about the same impact on him as the cold, which is to say none.

We're through the woods far faster than I would have been had I been alone, me following in the trail his big body blazes, and in less than three minutes' work on a back door that opens into the laundry room, we're inside.

Through the laundry room and two steps into the kitchen we're greeted by a barking, snarling black-and-brown beast of a Boerboel.

He is angry and aggressive and truly menacing

Harvey immediately breaks into song, performing something I vaguely recognize as a show tune, dance steps and all.

—*And now it's . . . springtime for Hitler and Germany. Deutschland is happy and gay. We're marching to a faster pace. Look out, here comes the master race.*

—The fuck you doin'? I ask.
—This has worked before.
—You've done this before?
—But that time I panicked and picked a number so pedestrian, so obvious, I wanted the dog to rip out my larynx.
—That what happened to your voice?
—Rawr. Kitty has claws. So mean to me.

The growling animal had momentarily looked confused

but that quickly turned to annoyance, then to anger.

    It is now steadily moving toward us.

    —I don't think it's working.

    —Guess I should've chosen something else.

    —Yeah, I say, 'cause that's the problem with your strategy—the song.

    —They say Hitler loved dogs . . . so I thought maybe they love him too. I had to try it.

    —Had to.

    When Harvey stops singing, the dog prepares to pounce.

    —Guess it was keeping him at bay, he says.

    The dog takes two leaping steps then bounds into the air, mouth open, angling toward little Harvey, but before it reaches its mark, Harvey draws back his massive oak-limb-like arm and swings his huge lighter-knot of a fist, punching the animal in the mouth with a devastating right hook.

    The dog lands a few feet away on the floor and doesn't move, just lies whimpering and shaking.

    —Sorry buddy, Harvey says. You should've just let me sing.

    He starts to say something else but his phone rings.

    Withdrawing it, he takes a look at the screen then answers.

    —Does he have an alarm *and* a dog? he asks.

    He waits.

    —Okay. Thanks sweetie.

    He ends the call.

    —Robin just rushed out of his office, he says to me. If we tripped an alarm and he has nothing to hide, deputies will be rolling up in just a few. If he's bent he'll come himself or send one of his little posse.

    —Let's take a quick look around and get out of here.

    We do and get nothing for our trouble. We're fast but reasonably thorough.

    —If the bastard has her, Harvey says, as we're passing the still-whimpering pooch on our way out, it ain't here.

—I know we were only in there for a few minutes, I say, but... did it strike you as too clean?

Harvey nods.

We are in the car heading back toward town.

—I don't mean the house was clean, I say. I mean that's not the house of a dirty cop.

—Maybe he ain't that kind of dirty, baby.

—What kind?

—The kind that'd have stuff to find. Illegal shit. Drugs. Porn. New and nice things—kind of things a clean cop couldn't afford. Maybe he's the kind that just does whatever the hell he wants to whoever the hell he wants.

—Or maybe we just missed it, I say. Maybe it's too well hidden for the kind of quick search we did.

—Or maybe that piece of shit old house is just his beard, baby.

—Interesting, I say. If he's got another place he could have her at it. You blowin' anybody in the clerk's office?

—No.

—That's too bad. I was—

—But I do have a cousin works there.

—Can she keep a secret?

—She kept mine for many years before I came out. Whatta we need?

—A list of all the property he owns.

While he calls her, I check in with Sylvia.

—How're you feelin'? I ask.

—Worried sick. Have you found her?

—Not yet, but not from lack of looking. You heard anything? Thought of anything else?

—I keep tryin' to but I'm useless. No good to anybody. And my little girl...

—We're gonna find her. You just rest so you'll feel good when we bring her home, okay?

—Thank you, Merrick. I'm so glad you came into our life.

When I end the call, Harvey is still on his so I wait.

—You sure? he's saying. Okay. Thank you darlin'.

He ends the call and shakes his head.

—That lovely home is all he owns, he says.

—Damn it. I thought for sure . . . Wait. Call her back.

He does.

—Ask her to see if there's anything in his parents' names, ex-wives, etcetera.

He does.

Then we wait while she does.

—Bingo baby, he says when he's off the phone again. B-I-N-G-O beautiful boy. There's a camp on the Brothers River still in his dad's name. And like mine, his daddy-o's dead as fuck.

Benny Wilson's camp on the banks of the Brothers River is only accessible by the waterway, which is why less than thirty minutes later we're heading toward it in a borrowed boat—this time out with Harvey's shotgun along for the ride.

We put in at Howard Creek among some of the oldest and largest and eerily shaped cypress trees I've ever seen, the sun setting behind us as we navigate around and in between their severely swollen and bloated bases.

—If I have to shoot and kill the sheriff, Harvey says, promise me we'll tell everyone it was a lovers' spat and a crime of passion.

—Deal.

It takes us far longer to negotiate the watery cypress swamp than it does to reach the camp once we're out on the river. The camp is one of the first you come to and we're pulling up to it minutes after clearing the trees.

—Well would you look at that, Harvey says. Someone's been here recently.

There in the damp bank just beyond the slap and tap of the rippling river water are tracks in the mud, the long, flat, squarish indentation of a boat and footprints.

A Certain Retribution

—Fuck. Wonder if we set off an alarm at his house that sent him here instead of there.

Harvey scans the area.

—No sign of anyone. Whoever was here is long gone now.

We climb out of the boat, Harvey with shotgun in hand, and rush up toward the small camp.

There is no lock on the door and no guard dog waiting inside.

There is also no Reggie.

The small, one-room shack has the look, feel, and smell of a simple, old-school fish camp. Several beds spread throughout the room. Some random furnishings. Decks of cards and board games. A few ice coolers. A collection of mismatched chairs around a fireplace.

The air is still and stale and smells of dusty dampness and mildew.

We look around for a few minutes.

And though it seems someone has been here, maybe even stayed here recently, there are no signs of foul play. No handcuffs dangling from bedposts. No drugs or gloves or gags on the bedside tables. No blood. No evidence to the quick inspection with the naked eye.

—Think he had her here and moved her? Harvey asks.

—Whatta you say we take your shotgun and go ask him?

—You sure about this? Harvey asks.

His voice is different now. Every bit as distinctive, but with none of the lightness, wantonness, or tomfuckery.

I nod.

We are driving back toward town from Howard Creek to find Robin Wilson and force him to tell us where Reggie is.

—You don't come back from something like this.

—I know.

—A criminal, even a civilian would be one thing, but a

sitting sheriff. . .

—Criminal with a badge is still a criminal, I say. And I think he'll be a civilian again soon, if FDLE has anything to do with it.

—Maybe, but right now he's the most powerful law enforcement officer in Gulf County.

I think about it.

—Even if he is unable to do anything official—like have us arrested or—he'll still retaliate.

—I know.

—Even if he is unable to retaliate for some reason—like, say, incarceration—he'll have one of his boys do it.

I nod.

—I'm not unaware of what we're about to do, I say. I was involved in something like this before.

—With a man like Robin? With a cop?

—No.

—Is she worth all this? The cowgirl. You sure she's—

—Yes.

—I'm just asking as your friend, just wanting to make sure you've thought it all through. Matters not to me my darlin' boy. I've got nothing to lose. I've been playin' with house money for more'n a minute, but you . . .

I've lost track of how long it's been by now, but Harvey has been HIV-positive for what seems like over a decade and a half now—and might actually be.

—What about the kids?

I nod.

—Keep thinkin' about them. Thing is, I had to do something not too dissimilar to this a few years ago for Casey. I know she'd understand—hell, demand that I did it for Reggie.

—But you don't have to, he says. You could just let me do it.

—I couldn't.

—You know the only way to really do it is kill him, right?

I shake my head.

—It's what we should do after he tells us what we need to know, but it's got to be something we're willing to do or it

won't work.
 I shake my head again.
 —Not a line I'm willing to cross.
 —Then take me home or let me do it alone.
 I glance over at him. Surprised.
 —You serious? I say.
 —I care about you too much to rush into something with you I know is doomed to fail, something that will come back so quickly to bite you in that cute little ass of yours. If you're not willing to kill him he'll know it, and then there's no real threat. Without that you've got nothing. He won't talk. You'll be forced to let him go and then he'll kill you. Or say he does talk. What then? You let him go? He's just gonna kill you or your kids.
 —There's got to be another way, I say.
 —Call me when you come up with it.

 We are just sitting down to dinner when there's a knock on the front door.
 —I'll get it, I say to Casey and Kevin. You two go ahead and start. Don't wait on me.
 I cross the small living room and open the door to find Rain, Reggie's sixteen-year-old son, standing on the stoop.
 He looks as if he's just come from football practice. Red athletic shorts with a faded white gator logo out of which his skinny, hairy white legs extend to grass-and-dirt soiled tube sox and well-worn cleats. His face is red and his unruly hair is still damp. The hoodie he's wearing is too big for him and hangs on his small frame as if borrowed from an athletic older brother.
 —Rain, I say. You okay? Is your mom—
 —I talk to you a minute? he asks.
 —Sure. Come in. You hungry?
 —Out here, he says, and steps down off the stoop and takes a few steps into the front yard.
 I follow.

—You have any idea where Mom is? he asks.

I shake my head.

—Tell me if you do. I want to know.

—I honestly don't.

—I'm worried about her.

—Me too, I say.

—Are you? How can you just be eating dinner like nothin's wrong?

—I looked for her all day, I say. I've got other people looking for her right now. I'm gonna look some more tonight as soon as I eat and check on Kevin and Casey.

He doesn't say anything, just lets his gaze drift over to the wooded wetlands across the narrow asphalt road.

Looking from him to his small, mud-covered Toyota truck with its ridiculous lift kit and enormous tires, I think it didn't take him long to fit right in here.

The dim evening is cooling off quickly as it fades into darkness headed toward night, and I feel a chill run up my arm and through my body.

—She's been through so much, he says.

I nod.

—She doesn't think I know, but I do.

I wonder what he knows but don't ask.

—Most of the bad shit that's happened to her was before I came along or back when I was a boy.

Casey comes to the door, looks out, nods, and closes it.

—I ain't gonna let anything else bad happen to her.

I don't say anything and he looks back at me.

—Well? he says.

—Well what?

—Where do I start? What do I do?

For all his sincere, well-meaning bravado, he's just a kid whose mom is missing, who's lost and doesn't know what to do, where to start.

—Take care of your grandma. I'll let you know as soon as I know anything.

—If someone has her, he says, I want to know. I want to be the one to go in and get her. I want to be the one to square

things. Understand?
　I nod.
　—I'm serious. I'm going into the military when I graduate. Gonna be a SEAL. I'm already in training. I can handle myself. I'm no joke.
　He grows quiet a moment and looks back toward the trees across the way, his eyes glistening.
　—She's my mom, you know? There's nothing I wouldn't do for her. You have any idea of what all she's done for me? It's gotta be me. I've got to be the one to . . .
　—I'll call you, I say. I promise.

　Restless sleep.
　Tossing and turning.
　Terrible, dispiriting dreams.
　Waking.
　Panic.
　Mistake.
　I should've listened to Harvey. Done what he said. If Reggie dies . . .
　Did I make a mistake? Was that the wrong decision? If I got to choose, I'd choose killing Robin over letting Reggie die, but was that my choice? By not being willing to kill him did I let her die?
　In one particularly bad dream I am telling Sylvia and Rain that Reggie is dead.
　They are crying and sobbing and screaming.
　—No! I want my mom, Rain yells. Where is she? What'd you do with her? She's dead because of you. Why? Why'd you kill her?
　Sylvia slowly, feebly pushing herself up, sheet sliding away to reveal her cancer-ravaged battlefield of a body.
　—I'm about to die, she says, her voice eerily airy, pathetically weak. She can't be dead. She can't die first. I've got to die knowing my baby is already dead. No. I can't. Please.

God. No. My baby. Not my baby girl.

And then she dies.

And then Rain is as distraught as any orphan I have ever seen, me offering to take care of him, him saying I was the last person on the planet he'd want to, that I had killed his mother.

I wake certain I've killed Reggie, wracked with guilt.

I doze fitfully again.

I wake certain of nothing, questioning everything.

Finally crawling out of bed, I dress and walk the short distance down the road and sit by Sylvia.

—You gonna be here a while? the hospice nurse asks.

I nod.

—Mind if I run back into town for cigarettes?

I shake my head.

—Always run out while I'm here. Strangest thing. Not a short trek to town either. It's been torture sitting here jonesin', but with how upset and agitated she is I just couldn't leave.

A little later, after the nurse is gone on her errand, Sylvia opens her eyes.

When she sees me her face grows alarmed, her eyes wide, and she begins to cry.

—You're here to tell me my baby's dead, aren't you?

—NO, I say. No. Just came to check on you, to sit with you. That's all. I swear.

—Oh my God, you scared me, she says, placing her bony hand on her chest.

—I'm so sorry.

—It's okay. It's so sweet of you. I'm just . . . I guess I'm just waiting for bad news, expecting to find out . . .

She doesn't finish and I'm grateful.

We sit in silence for a long moment. Eventually, she nods off and so do I.

I wake a short while later, look around, realize my phone is vibrating in my pocket.

Pulling it out I see it's Reggie's landline number from her office.

—Hello.

—Merrick?

A Certain Retribution

Her voice is soft and has the dry, unused groggy quality of someone having just roused from sleep.

I'm up immediately, rushing down the hallway, through the living room and out the door.

—Are you okay? I say. I'm on my way.
—Merrick?
—Yeah.
—I'm sorry.
—For what?

I run as fast as I can down Byrd Parker Drive, jump into my truck, and race toward Second Street and the old city hall building.

—For what? I ask again.

She doesn't respond.

—Reggie? Are you okay? Is anyone there with you?

She doesn't say anything, but I can hear her breathing and what sounds like placing the receiver on the desk near her because I can still hear her breathing.

I speed down the twisting, turning Lake Grove Road far faster than I should, flying past the nurse returning from town with her cigarettes, bouncing across the bridge at the Dead Lakes, nearly running off the road several times.

I find Reggie in her office, head resting on her arm next to the receiver on her desk. She is still wearing what she was when I saw her at Tucks some thirty-six hours ago.

—Hey, I say softly.

She rolls her head slightly, opens her eyes, and looks up at me groggily.

—Hey, she says, her voice sweet and sleepy.
—Are you okay?

She shakes her head.

—What happened? I ask. Where have you been?
—Take me home, she says.
—Did someone take you? Are you hurt?

173

—I think so.
—Which?
—Take me home. Please.
—Okay.

As I help her up, I try to examine her as best I can. There are no obvious signs of trauma or injury.

Her clothes look slept in and she acts drugged.

—Who did this to you? I ask.

I help her out of her office and into the main hall. She stumbles along, dragging her feet, bobbing her head about as if it's too heavy to hold upright.

—I don't know. I don't remember anything.
—What's the last thing you remember?
—Drinking at Tucks.
—That's it?

She nods.

—I think somebody drugged you, I say. I'm gonna call FDLE so they can examine you, determine what you were given and collect any evidence to see—

—NO, she says. Absolutely not.
—But—
—No.
—But it's our best chance at finding out what happened and catching who did it, and you know it.
—I don't care.
—Are you sure? It's important.
—I'm positive. And if you call them or tell anyone I'll never forgive you.
—Then I won't, I say.
—Take me home and take care of me.

—Whatta you think happened? Sylvia says.

I am sitting beside her bed. Reggie is asleep down the hall, Rain asleep on the floor outside her door.

—I can only imagine.

—Imagine.

—Something was put into one of her drinks. She was abducted. Most likely retaliation for something she did but it could be something else.

—Who?

—She has some small burn marks on her body.

—Burn marks?

—Consistent with being tased. She's only tased two men since she's been in town, and one of 'em's dead.

—Say his name, she says.

—Reggie tased Robin Wilson at the landing last Friday night when Donnie Ray Kemp's body was discovered.

—Just like high school all over again. Did he rape her?

—There's no evidence of it, but if it's him . . . he has a history.

—Biggest regret of my life, she says. Not doing something back then. I deserve to die. Did a long time ago.

—There's a chance she was just tased. Could be a way of exercising control over her, getting her back for the perceived insults and injuries. Maybe an attempt to scare her off the case.

—But how likely is that given his . . . history.

—Not very.

—I'm gonna kill him, Reggie says.

She is awake. We are in her bed.

In addition to taking care of her I've been helping the hospice nurse with Sylvia when I can and trying to help Rain process everything that is going on, and I'm extremely grateful I'm in here holding her when she wakes.

—Can't be certain it was him, I say.

—Certain enough for me, she says.

I wish again she would have agreed to let FDLE conduct an exam.

—His days are numbered, I say. He'll be arrested and convicted. You know what'll happen to a guy like him in prison?

—Maybe so, but in that scenario he's still drawing breath, still a living, breathing member of the human race.

—How're you feelin'? I ask, wanting to change the subject for a while.

—Weak. Defiled. Dirty. Disgusting. Ashamed. Embarrassed. Angry. I don't blame you for wanting to get as far away from me as possible.

—I don't.

—You will.

—I won't.

—Once it sinks in, when you've thought about what was done to me. I can't believe all that high and mighty shit I was sayin' about strippers. I'm so sorry. It's just insecurity. My body issues. My past. The way my ex treated me. Some of the things he did with strippers.

—I'm not your ex. I'm not going anywhere. You are the most beautiful woman in the world to me. I want you. I want you bad. When you're feeling up to it I'll prove it. Nothing anyone else does can defile us. Only what we do to ourselves. I'm just so glad to have you back. So grateful. I thought I had lost you. Just work on getting better. Rest. Relax. Just let everything go. Let me hold you. Let my love heal you.

—Your what?

—I love you, I say.

And she starts to cry.

Days have come and gone.

She is better.

She has slept more than she thought possible. She has bathed and gargled and douched and scrubbed and bleached about a thousand times.

Physically she is fine.

She and Merrick have made love many times—something that has helped her more than anything else.

She hasn't told him yet but she's in love.

A Certain Retribution

Perhaps the most surprising thing to come out of all of this, out of both her mom's illness and her own trauma, is the seismic shift in their relationship.

Her mom has apologized and explained and really seems to have changed.

—All we needed was a little death and abduction, Sylvia had said.

Reggie thinks it might actually be worth it to have her mom again.

—We've talked about me enough, Sylvia says. How are you feeling?

—Rested. Ready to get back to work.

Reggie is in the chair beside her mom's bed, as she has been so many hours over the past few days. The hospice nurse is on a cigarette run, Rain is in school, Merrick is helping his dad take the latest issue of the *Breeze* to press.

—How's your head?

—My head?

—Your thoughts? Your feelings? Your—

—A work in progress.

—Be careful there.

—Where?

—Your mind. Make sure it's not your master, only your slave. You're going to want to retaliate. Don't. It will destroy you. Don't let the jackals make you like them. Think of Rain. Think of your own soul. Listen to your mama.

She nods.

—I mean it. I know you. Right now you're wanting to put a boot on some throats. I'm begging you. Follow the law. Nothing less but nothing more.

—Aunt Reggie?

They both turn to see little Lexi Lee standing in the doorway.

—Hey baby, Sylvia says. How's my favorite granddaughter?

—How are you, Grandma? Sorry I haven't been by to see you lately.

—It's like looking at you at that age, Sylvia says.

It really is, Reggie thinks. She looks so much more like me than Becky.

—Is your mom here? Reggie asks.

—Just me. I need to talk to you.

—Sure, Reggie says.

Without saying anything else, she turns and walks back down the hallway.

—Must be a private talk she needs to have with you, Sylvia says.

Reggie finds Lexi Lee on the couch in the living room. When she sits down beside her, Lexi Lee turns and hugs her awkwardly.

—You okay? Reggie asks when she lets her go.

—I heard what happened to you.

—How?

—Mom. Grandma told her.

Reggie's anger flares and momentarily all the work of forgiveness and reconciliation with her mom is gone.

—How are you? Lexi Lee asks. You okay?

Reggie nods.

—I'm good, Lexi.

—I don't have long, she says. I snuck out of school.

—Why? What is it?

—That thing that happened to you. It happened to me.

—What thing? When?

—Mom was going to leave Dad. He hurt her one too many times or too much or something. Robin Wilson was going to help her. Arrest Dad. Help her get a place. They must've been . . . involved or something. I don't know. She asked me to stay with him while she packed up a few things and to tell him what all Dad had done. We were at his house to keep it all a secret. He gave me a soda and the next thing I knew I was waking up in my bed. Mom never mentioned anything. Just acted like everything with Dad was great again. It was all like a dream. A surreal dream with a nightmare inside of it.

—Robin drugged you?

—We're taught about roofies and how they make you feel and forget.

A Certain Retribution

—When was this?

—Before you moved back. Beginning of the summer.

—And your mother never said anything to you about any of it? Y'all never talked about what happened to you.

—I've never talked to anyone. You're the first. When I heard what happened to you . . .

—I'm glad you're tellin' me. And I'm so sorry for what happened—for all of it, your folks, your dad being an abuser, your mom staying, and for the horrific evil crime Robin committed against you, the unforgivable violation, the—

—I was a virgin when Mom dropped me off at his house, she says. When I woke up the next day in my bed, I wasn't.

When Robin crawls out of his sheriff's car in his driveway, Reggie steps out from behind one of the whispering pines on his property and drops him with her Taser.

While he's incapacitated, she removes the darts, kicks him in the nuts hard with her boots, cuffs him, and puts him in the backseat of her new patrol car.

—You couldn't've fucked up more if you tried, he says from the backseat, his voice still shaky, coming out in gasps.

She doesn't say anything, just keeps driving back toward town.

—You best kill me, bitch, he says, 'cause I ever get free I'm gonna burn your life to the ground.

She doesn't respond.

—You crazy fuckin' cunt. What's your plan exactly? You can't take me to my jail, and it's the only one in the county.

As she nears the end of Old Dairy Farm Road, she slows and looks out at the Listers' farm in the soft golden glow of sunset, wishing she was riding one of the handful of horses in the pasture behind the old dairy barn instead of dealing with the devil in her backseat.

—You best answer me, he says. I'm already tiring of

talkin' to myself. This is insane. You can't arrest me. I'm the sheriff for fuck sake. What's this about? Heard you were missing a few days. What happened? You wake up feelin' like somethin' big had been shoved inside you?

Thinking how she had felt no physical impact apart from the small Taser burns, she starts laughing.

She's grateful. Glad she can laugh. Glad she felt nothing physical to match the emotional and psychological trauma and violation she felt.

She laughs hard and long and in genuine amusement and great delight and it bothers him more than anything she could've said.

She recalls how she had nothing physical the morning after prom either, no soreness, no cuts or tears, no rips or contusions that typically accompany these type violations.

She wonders just how tiny his little dick is or if he can even get it up. Probably can't. Probably part of why he does what he does.

—Didn't feel a thing, she says. That's how I know it was you. Just like back in high school.

—I'm gonna show you how big it is, bitch, he says, spit slinging from his mouth, when I fuckin' break it off in you.

She keeps laughing. Genuinely. Authentically. Uncontrollably.

It's as cathartic as it is unexpected. A very real and needed release.

Then she thinks about Lexi Lee, what he did to her, and she is suddenly sober.

—You're a sick, twisted, corrupt criminal and rapist of women and children, and I'm going to do my job and protect the people under my watch from you.

He continues yelling obscenities at her. And threats. Kicking the seat. Writhing around like a caught animal in a cage.

She doesn't say another word to him. Just drives him to the old city hall on Second Street and locks him in one of the two old cells there that, until her arrival, had been used for storage.

—What's between us—your rape of me and my niece—

is personal, but what I'm doing is not. I'm doing my job. I'm going to do exactly what my mama told me to do—follow the law. Nothing more. Nothing less.

It's what separates us, she thinks. Why I don't retaliate, why I don't kill you or rape you with a nightstick right now.

—I'm going to call FDLE. Turn you over to them. That will end my duty as a police officer for this city, but as a person, as a plain ol' citizen, as a woman, hear me when I say if you ever come near me or any of my loved ones again, it won't be a Taser I put on you. It'll be a bullet between your eyes. I will not hesitate. I will not flinch. I will not stop shooting until you're unable to rape, exploit, harm, victimize, or injure another innocent person ever again.

Without waiting for a response, she walks out of the room, closing the large metal door, and down to the end of the small hall where she closes the old wooden hallway door and steps into her office. She calls FDLE.

After she finishes with FDLE and is assured special agents and techs are on their way from Tallahassee, she calls her mom.

—I have no idea how long this will take, she says.

—What? her mom asks. You weren't clear on where you were going or what you're doing.

—I've arrested Robin Wilson. I'm waiting for FDLE to come take custody of him. I'm doing just what you said. Following the law. Nothing more. Nothing less.

—I'm proud of you, baby. I know how trying this is. I know how tempting it is to . . . not to follow the law, but for Rain and Lexi and me and especially you, you'll be so glad you did. You're doing the right thing the right way. I love you.

—Love you. I'll probably be late. Let the nurse know and please keep Rain there. I don't want to have to worry about where he is.

—He hasn't come in yet, but when he does I won't let him leave again, Sylvia says. Don't worry about a thing here. Just be the amazing, strong woman of integrity I know you to be.

When she hangs up, she sits for a moment to gather herself.

Taking in a few deep breaths and letting them out slowly, she stretches and rolls her shoulders and neck.

She has a little over an hour until FDLE arrives.

What's my next move?

Find Allen Maddox. Not only is he most likely the homeless-looking man in the park the kids called a hobo, but he's very likely a witness to what happened to Donnie Ray.

If he can place Robin at the landing, she wants him here to tell FDLE that when they arrive.

Hell, he may even have seen him kill Donnie.

Of course there's another scenario, one she's tried not to think about too much. Allen could be the killer.

She hopes he's a witness to what happened and not the one who made it happen, but either way, she's got to find him. Taking one last deep breath and letting it out slowly, she stands and leaves her office to do just that.

I stop by Reggie's on my way home from helping get the paper out.

I'm tired, my eyes fatigued from looking at a computer monitor, my mind fried from the intensity of concentration and calculation, and my muscles are stiff and tense, especially in my shoulders.

A perfect night would include a long hot bath and making love with Reggie.

I'm surprised to find only Sylvia's old Chevy and Rain's fixer-upper Toyota truck in the yard when I arrive.

I figured Reggie was still resting, sleeping even. It surprises me and hurts a little that she didn't let me know she felt good enough to go somewhere. The only reason I hadn't called her was because checking on her was outweighed by not wanting to wake her.

I start not to even go in, but decide I should check on Sylvia.

Inside I find Rain making Ramen Noodles in the kitchen.

A Certain Retribution

—Hey man, I say. How was your day?

He mumbles something and shrugs.

—Where's your mom?

He shrugs again.

—No idea. Just got home. Stayed way late working on our homecoming float. It's so cool. Gonna be epic. Will win for sure.

—How's your grandma?

—Asleep.

—I'm gonna look in on her before I leave, okay?

—No problem.

I walk down the narrow hallway and into Sylvia's room to find her snoring airily.

I'm about to slip out to ask Rain where the hospice nurse is when she opens her eyes.

—Merrick, she says softly.

—Hey. How're you feeling?

—Weak as water but actually a little better I think.

—Where's your nurse?

—Caught her smoking inside the house. Sent her home. It's fine. I'm okay. Rain will be home in a little while.

—He's here.

—He is?

—In the kitchen, I say.

—Let me guess. Making Ramen?

I smile.

—Where is Reggie?

—You don't know? You haven't talked to her? She arrested Robin Wilson and is waiting for FDLE to come get him.

—Is Lexi Lee with you? Becky asks.

They are the first words Reggie hears when she answers her cell. No hello. No how are you.

—No, I'm out searching for a suspect. Why?

—I can't find her. She's supposed to be at Katlyn Jill's working on their homecoming float but she's not. One of the kids said she went to talk to you.

—I'll head back to my office and see if she's there. I'm not having any luck finding my witness anyway and it's almost time for me to be back.

—Call me the minute you get there. If she doesn't get home before Eric does . . .

When I arrive at the old city hall building, I don't see Reggie's car but decide to go in anyway.

Might give me a little time alone with Robin, another crack at getting him to admit something that'll help Reggie's case against him, another chance for one of his toxic leaks.

Entering the front door from Second Street by the fire station, I walk through the open room where the city commissioners have their meetings and where framed photographs of several decades of mayors hang on the wall, and head down the back hallway toward the old storage room that holds the cells.

The moment I turn the corner and step onto the wood floor of the hall, I know something is wrong.

I sense it. I feel it. I smell it.

Mixed with the musty mildewy smell of old, empty building is the pungent wet copper smell of blood.

Rushing down the hallway, I find the big iron door of the room open.

I stop suddenly to take it all in.

The cell on the left is empty, its door open about halfway.

In the cell on the right, Robin Wilson sits slumped against the back wall, dead.

Legs splayed out in front of him in a slowly expanding pool of blood, his body is pocked with more bullet holes than I can quickly count, several of them in his mangled and

A Certain Retribution

misshapen head and on his swollen, lifeless face.

On the floor outside of his cell, his gun lies on top of his leather belt.

—Killed with his own gun, I say. Reggie, what have you done?

My words, though spoken softly, ricochet through the room, bouncing around the cold, hard surfaces.

I sense someone behind me, feel movement.

I turn in time to catch the slightest glimpse of a man wielding something at me a split second before it hits me in the back of the head and—

As Reggie turns onto Osceola heading toward city hall, she sees Lexi Lee pulling out from behind the building and onto the road.

Stopping in the road, she motions for Lexi to roll down her window—something it doesn't appear she was planning to do.

—Your mom— What's wrong?

Lexi is visibly upset, tears streaking her cheeks, tremors running through the small, narrow frame of her body.

—What is it? Reggie asks again. Are you okay?

—What have I done? she says.

—What do you mean, baby? What's wrong?

The FDLE crime scene truck pulls up behind Reggie, followed by a car with two special agents, and Lexi speeds away.

Reggie yells after her but she doesn't stop.

Continuing to city hall to hand over Wilson to FDLE, she calls Becky.

—I just saw Lexi Lee. She's very upset. What happened?

—Nothing, she says. Nothing that I know of. I have no idea. I haven't seen her since she left for school this morning. Where is she?

—She's in her car. She just pulled onto Main Street.

—You didn't stop her?

—I tried. Look, FDLE is here. I can't leave right now. Find her and let me know what's going on. She's headed in your direction. Maybe she's coming home. Let me know. I mean it.

When I come to my hands are cuffed behind me and an FDLE crime tech is examining my head.

—I'm okay, I say. Help me up. Why am I cuffed?

—Get him up, Reggie says. Take him into my office.

As I am pulled up by two men on either side of me, I glance around to see that FDLE is already busy processing the Robin Wilson murder scene—making measurements, taking pictures, labeling, tagging, bagging.

—How long have I been out?

No one says anything. They just escort me into Reggie's office and leave. As soon as they do, Reggie and a thin redhead with skin paler than Robin's blood-drained body walk in and close the door.

—This is Maureen Evans. She's a special agent with FDLE. I'm gonna ask you some questions. She's going to observe. She knows we've been seeing each other, as do the other agents who walked in with me and found you.

I nod.

—What happened?

I told her.

—How long ago was that?

—I have no idea, I say. I don't know how long I was out.

—And the guy that knocked you out . . .

—I'd say the same one from Gaskin Park. The one Lonnie mentioned. Kids called a hobo. I only got a split second look at him but he didn't look homeless so much as unkempt.

—Did you shoot Robin?

My eyes grow wide and I start shaking my head.

—You really think—

—Just answer the question. Please.

—No. I did not.

—Do you have any idea who did?

—No. I do not. I came in and found him like that. I was in there less than a minute, maybe two, and got hit on the head.

—You satisfied? Reggie asks Maureen.

She nods.

—I'll give you two a minute, Maureen says and leaves the room, closing the door behind her.

—That's it? I ask.

—Pretty much, Reggie says.

She steps over behind me and cuts off the flex-cuffs from where my arms hang down between the back and seat of the folding metal chair.

I rub my wrists.

She returns to sitting on the front edge of her desk.

—Sorry, she says. Had to do all that for their benefit. I told them you didn't kill him, that you wouldn't.

—You never thought I did?

—Of course not, she says.

—Thank you.

—They confirmed you didn't with the SEM. Gunshot residue test with a scanning electron microscopy. They can tell you haven't fired a gun.

I nod and think about it.

—You not going to ask me if I did it? she says.

—No.

—Why?

—I know you didn't, I say.

—No you don't.

I smile.

—I honestly don't believe you did, I say.

—Well, no one else will when they hear about our history.

—Then don't tell them, I say.

She purses her lips and gives me a small frown.

—How the fuck did this happen? she says. How could I be so stupid? I should've never left him.

—Where'd you go?

—As it turns out, to look for the man who was probably

here killing him.

 —Seeing too much of each other lately, Sally Ann says.
Reggie nods.
 —I'm the one she's really gotta be sick of, Maureen says.
 —I'm grateful for you both, Reggie says. I truly am. Y'all mind if he's here?
 She nods toward me.
 —He's the closest thing to a deputy I have. Plus we're sleeping together and have no secrets.
 —That's pretty fast from suspect to investigator, Maureen says, but I've got no problem with it.
 —Me either, Sally Ann says.
 —I think the best way to proceed is for us to continue our investigation into Sheriff Wilson, Maureen says, and enfold the investigation into his murder into it. It's likely it's related. If it's not, it'll still be good for us to coordinate. We'll take the lead—especially since it occurred in your cell, don't want anyone claiming a cover-up—but we'll need your help and want you to be very active in it.
 Reggie nods.
 —Still can't believe I let it happen, she says. And in my own fuckin' jail cell.
 —Here's what we got, Sally Ann says. The killer, who is about Reggie's height or mine, and who is a very poor and shaky shot, empties Sheriff Wilson's entire .45 into the cell. He must've had one in the chamber 'cause we recovered nine casings and the weapon holds eight in the clip. It appears six went into the victim. Two or three after he was on the ground. At least one or two after he was dead or near dying. The killer then wiped down the weapon and didn't reholster it but set it on top of the belt. I'd say Robin was surprised by the attack—like he didn't expect it from the shooter. He was pretty close to the front of the cell at first. He must have held up his hands in a defensive gesture because one of the rounds went right through his right hand and into his chest. One of the rounds nicked his

carotid artery. We have arterial spray on the wall and ceiling. It's why there was so much blood. Why he got weak, slid down the back wall, and bled out—from that and the other holes in his body—slumping there as the shooter continued firing until the weapon was empty.

—So we got a shortish, shaky amateurish shooter who's committing an act of revenge, Reggie says. A crime of passion.

—Or a pro who wants it to look that way, Maureen says.

—So different from what was done to Donnie Ray, Reggie says. Is it possible it's the same shooter?

Sally Ann nods.

—Not in the manner of shooting, but in height, angle, trajectory, etcetera.

—You think it's the same shooter? Maureen asks.

Reggie shrugs.

—Just wondering if it could be. Lots of possibilities. Wilson could've killed Donnie Ray to cover his crimes, and somebody else for reasons unrelated could've killed him. Or the same shooter could've killed both to keep from being implicated in their crimes or for some reason we know nothing about yet.

—Not obvious or apparent, is it? Sally Ann says.

—Not to me, Reggie says.

—If it was easy, anybody could do it, Maureen says.

—Were y'all close to making an arrest? Reggie asks.

—Of Sheriff Wilson? Yeah.

—Who would he have been able to implicate if he cut a deal?

—Good question, Maureen says. The two names within his department that keep coming up as being involved in all his illegal activity are Skip Lester and Skeeter Hamm. Outside of his department there's plenty of corruption to go around. A couple of powerful and wealthy citizens, at least one county commissioner, and a congressman from Panama City. I haven't even really looked at them yet. They just came up in the investigation of Wilson. I'll get a list of names we can go over together.

Reggie nods then turns her attention to Sally Ann.

—Anything about Donnie Ray's or Robin's deaths that

make you think maybe Dahl Rogers wasn't a suicide? she asks.

Sally Ann shakes her head.

—No. I'm as certain as I can be that that was self-inflicted. I'm not saying they're not related. Just that he took his own life.

Maureen nods.

—His name kept coming up in the investigation. He was involved in some of the corruption. Thought he might cooperate, help us with the case. Help himself out. He took a different way out.

Reggie's phone rings. It's Becky.

—I need to take this, she says.

—Think we're done here for tonight anyway, Sally Ann says.

—We're heading back to Tallahassee, Maureen adds. Be in touch tomorrow. Get some rest. We're gonna need it.

Reggie waves to them and steps out of the building onto the front steps as she takes the call.

—Hey.

—I found her, Becky says. Finally got her calmed down. Gave her something to make her sleep. What the hell's goin' on?

—What'd she say?

—Nothin'. She never tells me anything. She was just upset. Crying. Babbling. What the hell happened?

—I have no idea. I just passed her and saw she was upset. Tried to get her to talk to me but she wouldn't. I need to talk to her.

—Why?

—Keep her home from school. I'll be by in the morning.

As Sally Ann and Maureen and the other FDLE techs are leaving and while Reggie is taking her call, I get a call of my own.

It's Harvey Harrison.

I walk to the front corner of the main room and answer.

A Certain Retribution

—Hey baby, he says. How's my handsome boy?

—Didn't think you were speaking to me, I say.

—Never not speaking to you, darlin'. Not ever. Besides, you were right. Good call. You got the girl back and the monster murdered without getting those sexy hands of yours the least bit dirty.

—What are you saying, Harvey?

—Just that you made the right decision. I know it wasn't an easy one to make. You got it right. I'm happy for you, honey.

—How'd you know Robin was dead?

—Oh and about that . . . encourage your girlfriend not to strain herself looking too hard for whoever did it. All they did was some community service, something needing doing, something no one else was willing to do.

—You sayin' what I think you're sayin'?

—Don't know. Whatta you think I'm sayin'?

—Harvey, who killed Robin Wilson?

—Whether it was that poor boy who wanders around town like he was in NAM or some shit like it, or one of his many victims, or . . . whoever it was, the lady chief's time 'twere better spent helping take out the rest of the trash rather than trying to find out who was just being helpful by taking out some himself . . . or herself.

The next morning after fielding phone calls from concerned citizens to outraged city commissioners to pushy reporters to the governor himself, Reggie drives to her sister's house after her husband has left for work.

—I'm lettin' her stay home from school today, Becky says.

—Good.

—She's still in bed.

—I'll just talk to her in there.

—What's all this about?

—That's what I'm trying to find out.

—Is she in some kind of trouble?

—Not that I'm aware of. All I want to do is help her.

—I suppose you think I'm as bad a mother as I am a daughter.

—I don't think either.

—It's not easy. Everyone's not as strong as you.

Reggie doesn't respond.

—Anyway . . . Just help yourself to my daughter. And be sure to tell me anything I might need to know, will you?

—Lexi. Lexi. Wake up. I need to talk to you.

Lexi Lee looks up groggily at her aunt, her expression moving quickly from recognition to happiness to alarm.

And then she pretends to fall back asleep.

—We have to talk, Reggie says. Do you want to do it here or at the station—or worse yet in Tallahassee at the FDLE office?

She slowly opens her eyes again.

—Sit up. Come on.

She rouses herself and props up on two pillows against the headboard, her body remaining mostly under the covers.

—I will help you, Reggie says. I'll take care of you, but I can't if you're not honest with me, if you don't tell me the truth. Understand?

She nods.

—Everything. You can't leave anything out.

—Okay.

—I mean it.

—Okay. I won't.

—What did you mean last night when you asked what you had done? What did you do?

—I meant the sheriff. I . . .

—What about him?

—Him dying. He deserved it. It's not that. I don't care about him. But it was so . . . terrible. All that blood. And the

way he looked. And the smell. Oh my God the smell.
—Tell me exactly what you did.
—I was looking for you. I thought you were there. I just went in looking for you. Heard something in the back. Figured that's where you were. Walked back there and . . . there he was.
—Who?
—The sheriff. Robin.
—What was he doing?
—Huh? Whatta you mean? He was dead. He was just sitting there dead. Sitting in his own blood. There was blood everywhere.
—He was dead when you went in?
—Duh. Why do you think I was so upset?
—What time was it?
—Don't know. Maybe twenty minutes before I saw you. Not sure.
—Was anyone in there? Did you see anyone at all?
—Just the sheriff.
—I thought you heard someone you thought was me back there?
She stops and thinks.
—I did. I thought I did.
—But no one was back there?
—Not that I saw. I was only in there for a minute. I ran out. Then I sat in my car and cried. Tried to pull myself together.
—Did you see anyone else come or go?
—No, but I was in the back. And I wasn't really looking. When I had it together enough to try to drive I pulled out and saw you.
—You seemed far more upset than just from seeing a dead body. As horrific as it was.
She nods.
—Guess so.
—Why?
She shrugs.
—Tell me.
She doesn't say anything.

—Why did you say, What have I done?

—I felt like it was my fault, she says. Like I shouldn't have told anyone.

—Who'd you tell? I thought you said you only told me.

—I . . . When I talked to you it was only you. I guess I thought . . . Did you kill him?

—Who else did you tell?

—I didn't mean to. I just got so upset. And then Mom made me mad. And . . .

—Lexi. Who?

—Dad. I told my dad everything. About Mom. About leaving. About what he did to me. Everything. So I thought if you didn't kill him, Dad did.

For the next few days, we search for both Allen Maddox and Eric Layton, Lexi Lee's dad, who hasn't been home since he left for work the morning after Robin's murder. We can find no sign of either of them. It's as if they've both vanished off the face of the earth.

The city commissioners hint that Reggie's job is in jeopardy and the governor, who has the task of appointing a replacement for Robin, hints around to see if she's interested in it.

The media is mostly unkind to Reggie, making fun of her, her police department, her using her own car and the old city hall building and the ancient jail cells that, until two months ago, had been used for storage for the past several decades.

None of it seems to phase her much, not even when they called her Paul Blart Mall Cop, which she actually laughs about.

A search of Robin Wilson's house conducted by FDLE turns up large amounts of GHB and Rohypnol, as well as a rape kit that includes latex gloves, condoms, lubricants, rope, tape, and tools.

—Talk this through with me, Reggie says.

A Certain Retribution

It's late. We are lying in her bed, our naked bodies entwined.

We have just made love and are sweating and satiated. Though it is another cold night, the trailer is warm for Sylvia—who, although weak, seems to be feeling better recently, and I can't help but believe it has something to do with her improved relationship with Reggie.

—What's that?

—What the hell is going on. 'Cause I can't get my head around it.

—Okay. Fire away.

—Dahl Rogers kills himself.

—Apparently.

—He was clearly mental and either involved with the corruption or knew enough about it that he posed a threat or they thought he did. They pressure, threaten, intimidate him. Who knows? But whatever his involvement in their corruption or their involvement in his demise, he pulled the trigger and killed himself.

—I'd say that's a fair assessment as far as conjecture goes.

—So his death has nothing to do with Donnie Ray's or Robin's, right?

—Not that we know. Not directly.

—So do theirs have anything to do with each other's?

—I'd say it's highly likely, but not necessarily.

—Same killer?

—Possibly, but not positively.

—Make a case for each, she says.

—Each what?

—Their deaths being connected and not being connected.

—Unconnected. FDLE is closing in. Donnie Ray knows where the bodies are. Robin kills him to keep him quiet. Or Donnie Ray is killed because he's a crooked cop and he was involved in something we don't even know about and it got him killed and it's unrelated to the investigation into Robin's department as well as their other criminal activities.

—So then why is Robin killed?

—Revenge for what he did to Lexi Lee if your brother-in-law did it. Revenge by or for another one of his victims? Or maybe for the same reason Donnie Ray was—cover-up. Maybe another member of the force or from their little posse is protecting himself or staging a coup and trying to take over.

—Maybe it's not just one, she says. Maybe it's both. Maybe it's Skip and Skeeter.

—Could be. That would fall under them being connected. They could also be connected if Allen Maddox did them both. Motive would be the same. Revenge. He was at both places. At least we think he was. He's getting back at them for what they did to y'all.

—Why wait so long?

—Have no idea and that argues against it being him or for that reason. But maybe seeing you stirred it all up for him.

—It's possible, she says. I hope it's not him. I'd rather it be Eric than him. As hard as that would be for the family, I think Lexi might be better off if he's sent away. Unless Becky just hooks up with another abuser.

—Which she has a better than average chance of doing.

—Still, I hope it's not Allen. I feel so bad for him.

—I know. Robin could've been killed by Harvey Harrison, I say, and explain.

—Wow. Didn't see that one coming.

—There's so much we don't see and don't know. And there's no way to. It's why it's so difficult to get your head around. Nothing wrong with your head.

—Nothin' wrong with yours either, she says, and reaches down and takes me in her hand.

—You're gonna have to stop doing that if you want to continue this conversation.

—Will you still love me if I lose my job? she asks.

—I will.

—Any ideas on what to do next?

—I was thinking a little oral and then intercourse, I say.

—I meant in the case.

—Then stop what you're doing and ask again.

A Certain Retribution

She stops what she's doing and says, Hey, I never asked you what happened with that hooker who was texting.

—Regan?

—Yeah. What'd she say? She want you back?

I nod.

—She thinks she does, I say.

Reggie pulls back a little. It's subtle—more to do with what can be seen behind her eyes than her actions—but it's there. And obvious for anyone looking for it.

—What'd you tell her?

—That the woman I love thinks strippers are nasty ass hookers, so I couldn't even be her friend.

—Really? she asks, brightening.

—Not verbatim, but yeah.

—You told her you didn't want to see her?

—I did. And that I was sorry but I couldn't even be her friend.

—What else?

—That I was in love with a cowgirl who wasn't speaking to me, but if I couldn't be with her I'd rather be alone.

She throws her arms around me and pulls me to her, my head pressing against her breasts, simultaneously maternal and erotic.

—You really did? she asks.

—I really did.

She releases me, pulls back, and looks me in the eye.

—Thank you.

—Just told the truth.

We are quiet a moment, looking at each other, breathing one another, finding the small, modest, mostly empty mobile home bedroom the best place on the planet.

—So, she says eventually, back to my question. What's the next move? In the case.

I think about it.

—Keep looking for Allen and Eric, of course, she says.

—Intercourse?

—I said of course.

—Oh.

And then it hits me.

—We should stake out Skip and Skeeter. If Allen is getting revenge, he'll go after them next.

—Oooh, she says. That's good.

—It's no slouch you're bangin'.

—You knoooow . . . she says, stretching it out playfully. We could start now.

We start with Skip only to discover that he's on duty.

We then make our way toward Skeeter's place, a houseboat on the river tied to a cypress tree on a waterfront lot in the back part of Red Bull Island.

The wooded lot is overgrown, thick with uncut underbrush, a narrow trail leading from Skeeter's truck to the plank bridging bank and boat.

We pass his place and continue down the dirt road past a few empty lots and park in one near the end.

—Not gonna be able to stake it out from a vehicle, she says. Let's go find a place to set up on his property.

—Sure, I say. What could go wrong with sneaking onto the property of a heavily armed paranoid redneck expecting trouble?

We walk along the road about fifty yards or so, then cut through the woods on an old logging trail.

The moon looms large and bright in the cloudless night sky. It's clear and cold, a clean easy-to-breathe crispness to the air that reminds me of a North Florida Christmas.

We're in the lot adjacent to Skeeter's, probably less than a hundred feet from his houseboat.

We're only about fifteen feet in when we come upon a parked car.

—Kids parking? I ask.

—Come on, she says, and starts running.

—What is it?

—That's Eric's car.

A Certain Retribution

He's been missing three days. Can't imagine there's any reason to rush. But I follow her like a dutiful deputy.

No longer needing to be quiet or go unseen, we jog down the dirt road, then the path to Skeeter's boat.

As we draw near, we can hear a static-streaked radio station playing country music loudly.

Reggie draws her gun and yells toward the boat without slowing down.

—Wewa Police Department. We're coming in. Do not shoot.

The homemade houseboat is rickety and leans to one side. Its roof is rusted tin, its walls of mismatched and mostly untreated wood. It sits atop a base of what must once have been a pontoon boat.

We find windows to carefully peek into before entering and through them we see what we've seen way too much of lately. Another dead body.

Skeeter Hamm sits in his ratty old recliner in a blood-soaked wife beater and blue jeans, a bullet hole in his left cheek and the center of his chest.

Reggie opens the door and slowly enters, gun first.

—ERIC, she yells over the George Strait song. IT'S ME. REGGIE. DON'T SHOOT. COME OUT. LET ME SEE YOU NOW.

There's no response and no sign of Eric.

Easing on into the small room, the first thing I do is locate the radio and silence it.

We then search the boat for Eric.

It doesn't take long.

There are only three rooms and Eric is in none of them.

—I'm gonna check the back porch, I say.

—Wait, she says. You're unarmed. Let me do it.

—Or you could just lend me your gun.

She laughs heartily at that.

We find Eric on the back porch.

He's wrapped in Visqueen and folded into the freezer.

Reggie looks at me and shakes her head.

—What the . . .

We step back inside and take another look at Skeeter.

He's just sitting in his recliner, slumped a bit perhaps but otherwise—apart from the blood and gunshot wounds—he could've dozed off while watching TV.

—I'm gonna call FDLE, she says. Again. But before I do, talk me through it.

—Okay. How about this? Eric comes to confront Skeeter, wants to see if he had anything to do with what Robin did to Lexi Lee.

—Or just assumes he has and comes to kill him.

—Or just beat the shit out of him, I say. Yeah. But Skeeter kills him. Wraps him up and sticks him in the freezer.

—So who killed Skeeter? she asks.

—That is the question. We know it wasn't Eric.

—How do we know that?

—He's been missing three days. Probably dead nearly that long. Certainly dead quite a while. Skeeter here was humming around until much more recently. He hasn't been dead nearly that long.

—FDLE will be able to give us a much better estimate of time of death, but you're right. I'd say he's been dead a day. Less maybe.

I nod.

—So who killed him? she asks.

—Same person who killed Robin and maybe even Donnie Ray, I say.

—Allen.

—Possibly. But it could've been one of the others we've mentioned. Or somebody we haven't.

—True.

—I bet whoever did it didn't even know Eric had been here and was in the freezer.

—I bet you're right.

—It's possible the same killer did them both, but why so far apart, and why put Eric in the freezer and leave Skeeter out here?

—Maybe Skeeter's been gone, she says. Maybe the killer was here waiting or maybe Eric was. Either way, he kills Eric,

wraps him up, and waits.
 —I think that's less likely, I say.
 She nods.
 —But the biggest question is, I say, what is it about the killer that would make Skeeter sit there and let him shoot him?
 —There's nothing threatening about Allen, she says.
 —Well, I say, at least nothing threatening-looking.

Without waiting for FDLE to arrive, Reggie and I race to find Skip Lester.
 She explained the situation when she called and said due to the imminent danger Lester was in, we would find him first, then meet them back at Hamm's houseboat.
 When Reggie calls the Gulf County Sheriff's Department dispatch she is told to go fuck herself.
 —Think they'll tell you? she asks.
 —I doubt it. Think it's pretty common knowledge that we are doin' it.
 She smiles.
 —Wish that's what we were doing right now, she says.
 —Me too, I say. I have an idea.
 —What? Do it while we look for him?
 —No, but that's good. I like it.
 —What was your idea?
 —Calling Dad and having him track Skip down.
 —That's good too.

—I ain't in any danger, Skip says. I assure you of that.
 We're in the parking lot in front of Listers' old hardware store on Highway 22, standing in front of our idling cars in the cold.
 All around us the empty town looks abandoned, eerily

empty sidewalk-lined streets beneath the alternating red-and-yellow glow of the flashing caution light dutifully flaring its warning into the cold, vacant night.

The two cars, their visible exhaust rising in the red glow of taillight, the low hum of their idling engines both lonely and menacing, add to the sense of sinister abandonment and dread.

—Like you give a fuck anyway, he says.

—We're tellin' you someone's killed Donnie Ray, Robin, and Skeeter, and you're tellin' us you're not in any danger?

He nods.

—I hope whoever it is comes for me, he says. By god I'll be the last person they come after.

Reggie looks at me.

—Do you understand what he's sayin'?

I nod.

—He's an invincible badass motherfucker who can't be killed but who welcomes all attempts.

—Just wanted to make sure I was getting it, she says.

—Were you?

She nods.

—I was, she says, and normally I'm no good with ambiguity.

—Maybe a small-town cop has time to stand around and make jokes, but I don't.

—Yeah, I say, that's something a small-county deputy would never have time for.

—I'm out of here, he says, and starts to turn.

—Wait, Reggie says. You got any idea who's killing your fellow fucknuts?

—It's not you? he asks.

She smiles.

—If it's not me.

—Nope. Can't say I do.

—Maybe he's not worried 'cause he's the killer, I say. Cleaning up messes. Tying up loose ends. Silencing witnesses.

—It ain't me, he says. But go ahead and look at me for it. I could give a fuck. It ain't me.

—You seen Allen Maddox lately? Reggie asks.

A Certain Retribution

—That dirty little dick motherfucker, he says.

—Careful how you talk about my old friend, she says.

He lets out a mean, harsh, humorless laugh.

—Some friend. You're one stupid bitch, you know that?

I step forward and his hand drops to his gun.

—It's okay, she says to me. Tell me why. Because I'm up here freezing my balls off trying to protect one of the men who raped me?

—No, he says. Because your old friend had a go at you that night like everybody else.

—Wha—

—If he's bumpin off bitches it's to keep his secret safe, not to defend his old friend's nonexistent honor.

—How are you? I ask.

She shrugs.

We are driving back toward Skeeter's houseboat.

—I love you, I say. I'm sorry.

She doesn't respond.

—He could be lying, I say. Probably is.

—I know, she says, but it would explain so much—both about Allen's behavior back then and what's happened to him since. But even if it's not true . . . just the way I keep having to be around motherfuckers like Skip, the way I'm constantly reliving it lately. It's . . . just too much.

—I'm so sorry, I say. On the upside it's in relation to untimely demises.

She laughs.

—True, she says. There is that.

The mood in the vehicle is noticeably lighter and we ride in silence enjoying it for a moment.

—Who knows, she says, maybe Skip and Allen will kill each other and this whole thing'll be over.

Sally Ann makes it short and sweet, confirming for us what we had suspected. Two different weapons. Two different killers. Two days apart. There was a struggle between Eric and Skeeter, and Skeeter killed him using a kitchen knife. There was no struggle two days later when Skeeter was shot while sitting in his chair. And like the murders of Donnie Ray and Robin, Skeeter's own gun had been used against him.

The next morning brings news as surprising and sad and wonderful as any we've received since all this began.

The governor appoints Skip Lester to serve out Robin's term. The Wewa city commissioners vote to dismantle their newly formed police department and give the contract back to the sheriff's department. And Sylvia's doctor declares her lymphoblastic leukemia in remission.

—You okay? I ask.

I find Reggie standing in her backyard looking out over the river.

She nods.

It's a bright, sunny day and the waves and ripples of the river sparkle. Across the way, on the bank on the other side, there's still a good bit of green mixed in with the browns and grays of early winter, and the sun seems to somehow find and highlight them.

—Mom's amazing news put everything else into perspective. Overshadows the crazy bad with crazy good. There's no comparison.

—It is great news, I say, but what the commissioners and governor did to you is—

—In no way surprising. Hell, I don't even blame them. I have blood on my hands.

—Only from cleaning up their mess.

—Haven't cleaned it up exactly, but . . . you're right. It's not my mess. I'm just mess adjacent.

I smile.

—The timing's pretty damn good too, she says. I moved back to take care of Mom. Looks like there won't be much need of that any longer.

—What are you going to do and do I get a say in it? I ask.

—It'd be one thing if we were further along in our . . . ah . . . association, but we can't make decisions based on such a new relationship.

—Why not? Speak for yourself. I can.

—Well, I can't. I have to consider Rain. My only job is to take care of him—be a mom and a dad. We'll probably go back to the Orlando area. Get my old job back. He can go to his old school and be with his friends again.

—Please stay.

—I can't. I'm sorry.

—I'm still in shock, Sylvia says.

—I know, Reggie says.

Still weak and now extremely fatigued, Sylvia is back in bed. Reggie, like so many times lately, is sitting in the chair next to it.

—But it's a gift. An unbelievable and unexpected gift. So unexpected. It's a second chance not just at life but at motherhood. I'm gonna be a better mama to you, baby. I promise. Sorry I didn't do it better the first time, but God is giving me a do-over and I'm gonna do it over right.

—We'll both do better.

—Just do me a favor, Sylvia says.

—What's that?

—Just don't rush off.

—I can't—

—I know you. You're gonna wanna leave again, but please don't. We need you. Think about what all our family has been through. Stay for Lexi Lee if no one else. Just stay. Stay for me. Stay and let's see what it's like living here without that damn forgetful chain-smoking angel of death nurse.

Reggie and I are walking up from the dock at the landing when Harvey Harrison pulls up in his colossal old 1969 Cadillac DeVille convertible.
—Hello handsome, he says.
—Hey, Reggie says.
We laugh.
—You are a handsome woman, darlin', he says. For a woman. But this fine ass son of a bitch . . .
Reggie steps in front of me.
—Is mine, she says. All mine.
—Are there no circumstances under which you'd let him blow me?
—Can't think of any.
—What if I told you I know where Allen Maddox is?
—I'd be tempted, she says.
—I wouldn't, I say. Sorry Harvey. No offense. And this isn't a decision either of you have anything to do with.
—You're sayin' we don't get any say in whose dick you suck? Reggie says to me.
—I think we should get a vote, Harvey says, and I vote me.
—Tell you what, Reggie says, you tell me where Allen is and I'll suck Merrick's dick.
—Do I get to watch?
—No. And that's the best deal you're gonna get, so take it.
—Okay, he says. If there's no better deal . . . I'll take it.
They shake on it.
We just stand there a moment, both of us looking at Harvey.
—Well? Reggie says.

A Certain Retribution

—Well what?
—Where is he?
—Can't help but think I could've gotten a better deal.
—Harvey, hurry. Tell me where he is. We don't want to lose him.
—We won't, he says.
—Why's that?
—Because, he says, nodding toward his huge car, he's in my trunk.

—We've been looking for you, Reggie says.
—I know, Allen says. I been hiding.
It's just the two of them. They are sitting across from one another at one of the cement picnic tables beneath a gazebo in Gaskin Park near the landing. His hands are bound behind him by metal cuffs with bright pink fur around them—the only kind Harvey had.
—That's not all you've been doing.
—Pretty much, he says.
—What about the other? Why'd you wait so long to get revenge?
—Revenge? I haven't, he says. You think I killed Robin and Donnie Ray for what they done to us? I didn't.
—You were seen at both scenes.
—I've been watching over you since you've been back, he says. I've stayed here in the park a lot. Wanted to be nearby when Robin and them tried anything.
—You sayin' you haven't killed anybody?
—I swear, Reggie. But . . .
—But what?
—I'll gladly take the fall for them if it'll help you. I mean it. I have no life anyway. I can say I did it if it'll get you out of a jam. Let me do it for you.
She shakes her head.
—I don't need you to do that. I just need the truth.

—I'm tellin' you the truth.
—Were you in the city hall building the night Robin was killed?
He nods.
—Doing what?
—Looking for you. I saw Robin all shot to shit. I was leaving when Merrick came in. I knocked him on the head and ran out.
—You knock him out down here too? she asks. The morning after Donnie Ray was killed.
He nods.
—You didn't kill Robin?
—No.
—No one would understand more than me, she says.
—I didn't. He was dead when I went in.
—Did you see anybody else there?
—Merrick. Your sister's girl was in her car in the back. That's it.
—Were you down here when Donnie Ray was killed?
—I was in the park, back in the woods. I try to sleep some when you're at work. I heard a couple of shots. I looked out at the landing and didn't see anything. You hear shots around here all the time—'specially this time of year, so I didn't think anything of it. But they sounded like they came from a handgun not a shotgun or rifle. Later I thought that was probably when he was shot. But his car wasn't at the landing, wasn't anywhere in sight. I went back to sleep. I got up and ate something later. Saw Lonnie come put his boat in and head downriver. A little while later I was back in the woods peeing. When I come out I saw the deputy car sitting there. I didn't realize it was empty at the time. Just thought it was parked.
—Did you see anybody in the car or getting out?
He shakes his head.
—I never saw Kenny Ardire put his boat in. Just his truck and trailer at some point. I didn't see another soul that entire evening until y'all got here later that night, except for a black man in a pickup drive up and turn around—didn't even get out of his truck—and a kid in a black hoodie with

something white on it kinda loping down Byrd Parker at some point.
    —Did you see the kid before or after Donnie Ray's car was left at the landing?
    —Can't be sure. After I think.
    —Could it have been right after? Could he have been walking away after dropping the car?
    He shrugs.
    —I guess.
    —It's important.
    —I can't be sure.
    —You said something white on it, she says. What do you mean?
    —Couldn't make it out. Too far away. Was a solid black hoodie with something white on the top back right just below the shoulder.
    —Allen, did you rape me the night of our prom?
    Tears fill his eyes instantly.
    —I . . . who . . .
    —Skip Lester said you did. Said you took a turn at me just like the rest of 'em.
    —Robin held a gun to my head while they did what they did. I . . . I tried to fight them off, tried to . . . I was drugged too. Just didn't have as much as you because I was driving us and mostly pretended to drink. I was out of it though. I wish I'd've just made him kill me. He just kept sayin' if I didn't he'd shoot you too. When they finished he told me I had to do it. If I didn't, if they couldn't implicate me too they'd just kill us both. They pulled my clothes off. I was so scared, so embarrassed, so . . . goddamn powerless. I got down on the ground with you and just sort of hugged you. But they were havin' none of that. They . . . I told them I couldn't do it . . . couldn't get it up. They mocked me. Laughed and jeered. They . . . it was . . . Robin said if I didn't at least rub my little limp dick against your pussy he'd put another hole in you with his gun and they'd all take turns fuckin' it. So I did. I didn't go inside you. I didn't . . . All I did was sort of rub against you for just a minute. I . . .
    —I'm so sorry, she says. I had no idea it was so much

more traumatic for you. I wish you would've told me. I wish. . .

—I . . . I felt so bad . . . so guilty. I tried so hard not to . . . but . . . I started gettin' . . . gettin' . . . you know . . . erect and . . . I couldn't help it. There you were laying there having just been raped by these assholes and I'm getting turned on.

—You were a teenage virgin rubbing yourself against a girl, Reggie says. Of course you got turned on.

—I didn't . . . I didn't do anything. I mean . . . I didn't stick it inside you or anything . . . but I wanted to.

—That's understandable. And noble.

—I've always felt far worse about that than anything else that happened.

—You're just gonna let him go? Harvey says. Just like that? You doin' a sister wrong, girl. I work so hard to find him and then . . .

—He didn't do it, Reggie says.

The three of us are standing out of earshot of Allen, who is sitting in the passenger seat of Harvey's Caddy, awaiting a ride back into town.

—And even if he did, she adds, I'm not a cop anymore.

—Cop or not, I say, if you thought he did it, you wouldn't be letting him go.

She shrugs.

—Honn-neey, Harvey says. Think about who was killed. Who cares? Really.

—And there's that, she says.

—You sayin' you're done looking for the killer? I say.

She smiles.

—Didn't say that exactly, now did I?

—So, Harvey says, if he didn't do it, who did?

—I still like you for it, I say.

—Me? Really? Baaa-byyy. How exciting. Beautiful, haunted gay man kills corrupt redneck cops for small-town justice. I like it. Who do you think would play me in the

Lifetime movie? Oooh. Merrick, you could write the book.
—You sayin' you didn't? I ask.
—What was it exactly that gave it away that a gay guy was the doer?
—Pink bullet casings.
—I didn't even know about any of this until you showed up on my church house doorstep. It's a stretch but maybe I could see me doin' Robin, but the rest, really?
I shrug.
—Yeah, I say. Guess you're right.
—You sure it's not Captain Needs-A-Bath in my car over there?
—As positive as I can be, Reggie says.
—If it's not him and it's not me, Harvey says, who the hell is it?
—Wish to hell I knew, she says. But at this point I'm thinkin' it might go unsolved.
We are quiet a moment.
—You got any ideas? she asks me.
—Maybe it's what we said before. Skip took out anybody who could connect him to the crimes and corruptions and got a new job in the process.

Thanksgiving morning.
A perfect day. Clear. Cool. Bright. Perfect.
Two days before, on a cold, wet, gray Tuesday, their family had laid Eric Layton to rest. In some ways Lexi Lee had looked relieved, but Becky had acted the fool, pretending the controlling, abusive prick had been a good man and would be missed.
Reggie is in her mom's small kitchen cooking and counting her blessings.
There's Rain, of course. Mom being better. Merrick. Merrick's cock.
And thus ends the list— Not because there is not more

to be thankful for but because now all she can think about is his big, beautiful cock.

Now, horny as hell, she's thinking the cooking can wait, thinking maybe Thanksgiving dinner instead of lunch.

Her phone rings. It's him. Perfect timing.

—Did you hear? he says.

—Whatta you doin' right now? she asks.

—Helping Casey cook. Well, more sort of watching Casey cook. Lending moral support.

—So she can spare you?

—Sure. You didn't answer. Did you hear?

—Hear what?

—They found Skip Lester dead this morning. He was murdered last night. Shot with his own gun.

—What?

—Were we wrong about Allen?

—That's sweet but it wasn't we. It was me. And no. I don't think so.

—Well then who—

The front door opens and Rain walks in with his girlfriend.

—Gotta go, she says, cutting Merrick off. Call you back.

Rain is wearing a black hoodie.

She drops her phone when he turns to take off his shoes and she sees a white patch of paint on the upper right shoulder blade area.

Her heart seems to stop with the catch of her breath and her knees buckle a bit. Catching herself by the countertop, she seeks equilibrium but there's none to be had.

—Morning Mom, he says. We're gonna say hey to Grandma and go to my room. Smells good.

—Wait.

He stops and turns from halfway across the living room, the little pixie trailing him bumping into his back.

—Where were you last night?

—Told you. Spent the night with Geoff.

Her phone rings.

—Just wait a minute, she says to him, and takes the call.

A Certain Retribution

—Please hold the line for Governor Grantham.

She doesn't respond, just does as she is told.

—Reggie, I should've appointed you sheriff. I was wrong. I am sorry. Would you please do me the favor of accepting the position now? It's a mess—one that just got bigger today, but I'm confident you can clean it up. Whatta you say?

—Can I get back with you later today? she says.

Without waiting for a response, she ends the call and returns her attention to Rain.

—Where'd you get that hoodie? she asks. Why haven't I seen it? How long have you had it?

—Why? Traded a kid at school my old slides for it. I was cold.

—When?

—I don't know. A while back. Not very observant for a cop.

—You haven't worn it a lot lately, his girlfriend says. He hasn't worn it a lot lately. There for a while, he was wearing it all the time.

—We finished playing my hoodie history? he asks. Can I go say hey to Grandma?

She nods.

Always just been the two of us. My little man. Did he find out what had happened to me and decide to get revenge?

Turning off the burners in use on the stove, she rushes to her room to check her files.

Removing the key from the small collection of coins, random earrings, and buttons in the tiny ceramic bowl Rain made her for Mother's Day a few years back, she scolds herself for not hiding it better.

Unlocking the metal file box, she can tell immediately someone besides her has been through it.

Think.

What do I do? What have I done?

I can't . . .

Think, goddamn it.

Okay. Allen heard the shots but didn't see anything in

213

the landing—not even Donnie Ray's car. Was he here? Did Rain shoot him here then drive his car to the landing?

Shit, it fits.

She thinks back to what Sally Ann said about Donnie Ray. *Best I can tell the victim was shot once at close range. ME investigator said there's an exit wound so we're probably not going to have the projectile for analysis unless it turns up where he was shot. There's no sign of it here—either at the landing or where the body was discovered.*

Look for the slug.

She begins inside. Checking the ceiling and walls in every room. Nothing.

Outside. Out front. Nothing in the trailer or the trees. No sign a weapon was fired anywhere out here.

But as she walks toward the back she suddenly knows what she will find.

And she does.

Down by the river in the bark of a cypress tree. There it is.

She looks at it but doesn't touch it, doesn't remove it.

So he shoots Donnie Ray here. Rolls his body into the river. Drives his car to the landing. Is seen by Allen as he walks back.

My son is a murderer.

Your son is a serial murderer.

He's killed so many people.

She collapses, her body crumpling into the wooden porch swing mounted between a frame of three beams in the yard.

How can this be?

The day is too beautiful, too perfect for anything bad to happen, for her to discover that her son is the killer she's been searching for.

Please God no.

Lost. Scared. Devastated. Mind racing, reeling, recoiling from what's confronting her.

Who do I talk to? Who do I tell?

No one. Not a soul.

A Certain Retribution

    I can't bear this alone. Can't figure out what to do by myself.
    Yes you can. You've always been by yourself. You always take care of everything. Make all the hard choices.
    Do I turn him in? I can't.
    You can't not. He's a . . . he's killed four people.
    The four fuckers who raped his mom.
    Still. Four people. Four people you didn't kill. Why didn't you kill them? You wouldn't but you're going to let him?
    —I thought I was dying.
    Reggie turns to see her mom standing behind her.
    —Huh?
    —I saw you looking at the files, then out here. What'd you find?
    —What?
    Her mom steps around and sits down beside her on the swing.
    —Is it evidence of some kind?
    —I don't understand, Reggie says, her mind reeling. You?
    —I thought I was dying, she says again. As I was asking myself what good I could do with the little time I had left I heard you telling Merrick about what happened, who did it, and how your dad and I failed you. I knew then what I would do. What your dad should've done back then. What's that old proverb about he who seeks revenge should dig two graves . . . well, mine was already dug so . . .
    —You killed all four men?
    —Wicked men who stole and raped and murdered . . . who molested little girls and . . . Who was gonna make them pay? Who? They're like Washington only worse. They make their own rules, do what they want, and never get punished for anything. Men . . . men who weren't just part of the system. They ran it. They were it. Think about how corrupt, how crooked and evil all of 'em are. Including your ex. Men . . . surrounded by other corrupt men doing whatever the hell they want to women and children and other decent, weaker men. They did just what they wanted to, treated my daughter and granddaughter like . . . worse than their goddamn huntin' dogs.

—But you killed four men.

—With their own guns. None of 'em figured a frail old lady for a threat. Not even after they all started being picked off. Robin was the easiest, but none of 'em were hard.

—But—

—I love you, baby. I'm so sorry for being so weak, for not protecting you like a mother should, for not taking care of you the way you do Rain. I never thought I'd get them all. Donnie Ray was parked out front. Watching the house. Harassing us. I saw an opportunity. That damn nurse went to town for cigarettes and I went out front. Motioned him over. Told him I thought I saw something out back in the water and . . . when he fell into the river and began floating I decided to move his car, thinking maybe he would float so far downstream I might just get away with it. If he died. He was still alive when he went in but he didn't look like he had long.

—That's why he didn't sink, Reggie says. He was alive when he went into the water. Still had air in his lungs.

—I went inside. Grabbed Rain's jackety thing, put the hood up, drove the car over, and walked back.

Reggie nods.

—What did you find back here? Sylvia asks. What made you look in the first place?

—The projectile. It went through Donnie Ray and into that tree.

—There are probably a few more. I didn't hit him the first two times. What made you look in the first place? Did I do something to the files? I tried to put them back just the way they were.

—The hoodie. Allen saw you walking back from parking the car at the landing.

—I wasn't going to let that poor boy take the fall for what I had done. My plan all along was to tell you, to turn myself in—if I didn't get caught, which I figured I would. If you had arrested anyone, I would've stepped forward. But as long as you didn't, I intended to get them all. Then I got the shocking news. Remission. I couldn't believe it. I . . . I know you won't believe it—no one will—but I think what I did made me better. Doing something. Taking action against . . . Standing up for my baby girl. And then our relationship started getting better. And I thought . . . maybe I will get away with it. Maybe it will go unsolved and we can be what we never were before.

—I just can't believe . . .

—I'm not sorry for what I've done. Even after I learned I was in remission, I wasn't sorry I did it. Not for one second. I'm not a bad person. People like them shouldn't be free, shouldn't be walking around, shouldn't be hurting others. I should've done this years ago. If I had, Lexi Lee wouldn't've have had to go through what she did. Think about it. Just imagine what he did to her.

—I don't have to.

—That's right. That's why shooting Robin felt the best. Goddamn but he had that coming. I'm not saying I derived any pleasure out of putting any of 'em down. I didn't. It was just something that needed to be done. But with Robin I really felt like I was saving other young girls, like I was making the future world better somehow.

—I called you and told you he was there, Reggie says. You were the only one who knew.

—Your call was considerate. Innocent. Has nothing to do with what I did.

—How'd you get to him with no one knowing?

—That stupid nicotine-addicted nurse was going for cigarettes so I gave her a long list of things to get me from the Dollar Store. I drove up there while you were out looking for Allen. I did it and was back in bed before anybody even knew he was dead.

—The other two?

—Same with both. Told them I was very worried about you and what you were about to do and needed to talk to them about it. They welcomed me in like their own mamas.

And it was as a mama she was going in.

—You really don't feel guilty? Reggie asks.

—I don't. I know I broke the law. But I don't think I did anything wrong. If someone did something to Rain and you were dying . . . you wouldn't do the same thing?

Reggie shrugs.

She thinks back to just a few short minutes ago when she thought Rain might be the killer and how she had no intention of turning him in if he was.

—I honestly don't know. Not sure what I would do.

—What will you do with me?

—Wearing the badge means something to me, she says.

—I know.

—It's sacred. It's a trust. I can't explain it exactly. It's like it's so much bigger than me that my own personal preferences, prejudices, paybacks become irrelevant.

—You're not wearing the badge right now, Sylvia says.

—But I hope to again.

Sylvia nods.

—I'm not saying what I'm gonna do, Reggie says. 'Cause I honestly don't know. Just tellin' you what is true for me.

—I know. And I'm so proud of you. I truly am. I don't tell you enough. What you've done. What you've become. What you've done with Rain. You're an amazing woman. I'll gladly accept whatever you determine. I know you'll know what to do.

—What do I do? Reggie says.

—Are you absolutely certain it was her?

She nods.

—I just can't believe it.

—Blindsided me a little too.

—I can't tell you what you should do, I say.

—Do I take Rain's grandmother away from him? Rob him of the extra time we were just given? Can I let a multiple murderer go free? How can I? I wouldn't even consider it if it were anybody else.

—Thank you, I say.

—For what?

—Trusting me. It's huge.

—It is, isn't it? she says. I'd call that progress.

A Certain Retribution

—Unless . . . you just told me hoping I'd turn her in so you don't have to.

She laughs.

—Damn. Damn. Damn. I like the way you think.

I smile.

—Tell me what to do.

—Can't. Sorry.

—Talk me through it.

—Violate something that is sacred to you, deny who you are, refuse to ever wear the badge again and let her walk, or turn her in and deny you your mother and your son his grandmother and become the talk not just of the town but of . . . well, who knows, maybe the country. Both will cost you plenty.

She nods.

—No matter what you do you're going to pay with part of your soul.

She nods again and wanders off in thought for a while.

I can tell when she's made her decision. The making of it has a palpable impact on her entire being.

—Both decisions will cost me but only one will cost Rain.

I nod.

—It's as a mother you're deciding what to do about what your mother has done.

—What she did, she did as a mom—and a grandmother.

We sit in silence for a long moment.

—What about us? I ask.

—Think what I've shared with you, the trust I've given you, says it all.

—Say it anyway, I say.

—I love you, she says.

It is the first time she tells me.

—And? I say.

—And?

—And you're not going anywhere.

—And I'm not going anywhere, but . . .

—But?

—I'm gonna need help finding a job after I tell the

governor I can't accept his appointment.
—We'll figure it out, I say.
—You know, she says, I actually believe we will.

Sylvia doesn't say anything when she hears the news.
—Mom? Reggie asks.
—Yeah?
—Are you relieved? Are you—
—I'm . . .
Eyes unfocussed, face expressionless, she stares blankly ahead.
—I'm not sure what I am. I'm . . . sitting here trying to . . . figure out what I feel. It's the strangest thing.
—Are you okay?
—It's not the decision I thought you would make, she says, her gaze still fixed in the distance.
—Me either, honestly.
—Why did you? she says. I wouldn't tell people why I did it. No one would have to know.
—Everyone would know. It would all come out. Every bit of it plus a whole lot of made-up shit, but that's not why I did it.
—You know I'd understand, don't you darlin'. I told you, I expected you to arrest me.
—I'm doing it mostly for Rain.
Sylvia's face softens, her mouth forming the first hint of a smile, as she nods her understanding and approval.
—We'd all pay dearly for it, Reggie says, but I'm afraid it'd exact the biggest sum from him.
—Then you made the right choice. I'm so sorry I put you in this position. I never meant to. I honestly didn't even think I'd finish the job before I died. I did it for you. It was long overdue. I'm sorry. But I never intended for you to find out. Let alone have to deal with it, have to make all these decisions for all of us. I've burdened you again. Seems all I ever do. I'm so sorry,

baby.

They are quiet a long moment.
—Will you tell me something? Sylvia asks.
—What's that?
—Are you glad I did it? Are you glad they're gone?
—That's something I've been trying not to think too hard about.
—Why's that?
—I'm afraid I just might be.

We make love late that night in her bed after Sylvia and Rain are fast asleep.

And it's different somehow.

I'm not even sure how exactly.

It's not that our bodies are still full of leftovers and a bit sluggish from a holiday spent mostly sitting around talking and playing games with the kids. In fact, it has nothing to do with our bodies at all.

It's psychological and spiritual and subtle.

It's as if we're a little removed from what's taking place, almost but not quite like we are more observers than participants, as if every touch is a little too tender, every word slightly muffled, and I wonder if it's shock and exhaustion or part of the price Reggie is already paying.

Is this an anomaly or a new norm?

It's still good—very good—but it's different, and though slight, different enough to be noticeable, nagging.

It's like Reggie has retreated a short distance within herself. I can still reach her but not as well. It's as if she's just a little distracted, like someone paying partial attention to what I'm saying.

Later that night Reggie bolts up in bed beside me.

I'm awake instantly. Alert. Aware. Accessing.

I reach over and snap on the lamp on the bedside table.

—Bad dream? I ask, putting my arms around her.

She shakes her head.

—What is it?

—I can't do it.

—What?

—I can't not turn her in. I thought I could, but I can't. I'm not her. I'm not a vigilante. I couldn't have done what she did and I can't cover it up. I can't be an accomplice. And I don't mean in the legal sense, though I guess that applies too.

I nod.

—Do you understand?

—I do.

—Am I wrong?

—No, I say, shaking my head firmly.

—Would I have been if I had been able to not turn her in?

—Yes.

—But you wouldn't have said anything?

—Right.

—I love you.

—I actually think you do.

—You gonna walk through this nightmare with me?

I nod.

—I'm not going anywhere.

—Unless my mom shoots you.

I smile, appreciating her humor.

—Unless that.

—You sure you don't want me to go in with you? I ask.

It's early the next morning. Reggie and I are sitting up in bed.

She is trying to prepare herself to go in and tell her mom

A Certain Retribution

that she's changed her mind.
　—Thank you but it's got to be me and I've got to be alone.
　I nod.
　—But . . .
　—Yeah?
　—Will you wait here until I'm done?
　—Of course. I'll be right here.
　She nods and stands.
　—Last time I'll ask, I say. Are you sure?
　—Wish I wasn't, but I am. Certain.

　She returns so fast I conclude she was unable to tell her. But when I see her face, I know better.
　—She's not in her room.
　Jumping up, I hop out of the bed, meeting her between it and the door.
　—Are you okay? I ask.
　She shrugs. There are tears in her eyes.
　—She wasn't in her room but this was.
　She hands me a single folded sheet of copy paper.
　I take it. Unfold and read it.
　I know my girl. There's no way this would work. It's just a matter of time before you realize what you have to do, which lets me know what I have to go ahead and do now. I've put you through enough. No more. And nothing for Rain. This is how it was supposed to be all along. All I'm doing is following the original plan. And it's so easy. Just a little accidental overdose. Happens all the time. Clean up this one last mess for me honey and then give all the time and love and attention you've been giving to me to Rain, being a great sheriff, and making it work with Merrick. I'm so proud of you. Sorry I didn't do better by you but you turned out amazing just the same. All my love. Mom.
　I take her in my arms, dropping the note as I do, our bodies pressing into one another as the single sheet of paper flutters to the floor.

—I love you, I say. I'm here. Not going anywhere. How do you feel? I'm so sorry.

—Turns out she was far more brave than I realized, she says.

—We knew you had to get it from somewhere.

—We've got to find her, she says. What if she's out—

She turns and rushes from the room.

I follow.

We only make it as far as the end of the hallway.

From there we see Sylvia sitting at the kitchen table eating pancakes with Rain and Lexi Lee.

—Did we wake you? Sylvia asks. We've been trying to be quiet. You two want pancakes? We've got plenty. These two are lightweights.

—Not me, Rain says. I'm just gettin' started. Know what I mean?

Sylvia obviously sees something in Reggie's expression.

—You saw my note, she says.

Reggie nods, as we cross the room.

—Sorry honey. I just couldn't do it. I couldn't miss one second of this that I didn't have to.

—I'm so glad, Reggie says. I don't want you to miss a single second of this, of them, of us, of life.

Rain and Lexi Lee, eating pancakes and on their phones, are oblivious to everything else.

—But you won't be able to—

—Yes I will. I can live with this. I'm not sayin' it'll always be easy, but . . . you have my word.

—You sure?

—Certain.

—Then y'all pull up a chair and have some of Sylvia's famous chocolate chip pancakes.

A Certain Retribution

—Do I tell you I love you too much? I ask.

Reggie and I are sitting on the dock at the end of the road in the last light of late evening, the Apalachicola swirling by, reflecting the clear blue sky above it.

—Is that a trick question? she asks.

Her head is on my shoulder. We're both staring forward, gazing out at the gloom, looking before we lose the light.

—All I want to do is tell you, I say. I feel like I say it all the time.

—You say it a lot, she says.

—Too much?

—Whoa there, partner. Slow your gallop a bit. I didn't say that.

I smile.

We sit in silence for a while.

In the receding light the nocturnal noises of the swamps that are sacred to me begin to hum, as if an orchestra warming up for a night concert.

Life lately has been demanding but not overly difficult—and filled with far more normality than I would have guessed it would be.

I've focused on supporting Reggie in her decision—talking her through it, talking her off the ledge a time or two.

I also encouraged her to accept the governor's appointment, which she eventually did, becoming the first female sheriff of Gulf County.

Being both a sheriff and an accomplice after the fact to a string of murders is difficult for Reggie, but she's resolved, and I can tell she will stick with it, live with the contradiction, reconcile as best she can the dichotomy both decisions represent.

FDLE continues to investigate the deaths of Robin and his corrupt deputies but no new leads have turned up. And in spite of everything or perhaps because of it, Reggie and I are still pressing into each other, still gratefully accepting the gift we've been given of one another every single second we get together, having just been reminded how temporal and capricious everything in life but love can be.

Michael Lister

—Didn't you have something you wanted to say to me? she asks.

I smile and nod.

—Well? she says. What was it?

—You know, I say.

—I just might but I want to hear you say it.

I nod.

—Makes sense, I say.

—So?

—So I wanted to tell you what I always want to tell you, what I sometimes stop myself from telling you for fear it is too much and will scare you away.

—And what is that exactly? she asks.

—Just this, I say.

She smiles.

—I love you.

About Michael

Multi-award-winning novelist Michael Lister is a native Floridian best known for literary suspense thrillers and mysteries.

The Florida Book Review says that "Vintage Michael Lister is poetic prose, exquisitely set scenes, characters who are damaged and faulty," and Michael Koryta says, "If you like crime writing with depth, suspense, and sterling prose, you should be reading Michael Lister," while Publisher's Weekly adds, "Lister's hard-edged prose ranks with the best of contemporary noir fiction."

Michael grew up in North Florida near the Gulf of Mexico and the Apalachicola River in a small town world famous for tupelo honey.

Truly a regional writer, North Florida is his beat.

In the early 90s, Michael became the youngest chaplain within the Florida Department of Corrections. For nearly a decade, he served as a contract, staff, then senior chaplain at three different facilities in the Panhandle of Florida—a unique experience that led to his first novel, 1997's critically acclaimed, POWER IN THE BLOOD. It was the first in a series of popular and celebrated novels featuring ex-cop turned prison chaplain, John Jordan. Of the John Jordan series, Michael Connelly says, "Michael Lister may be the author of the most unique series running in mystery fiction. It crackles with tension and authenticity," while Julia Spencer-Fleming adds, "Michael Lister writes one of the most ambitious and unusual crime fiction series going. See what crime fiction is capable of."

Other John Jordan novels include RIVERS TO BLOOD, THE BODY AND THE BLOOD, BLOOD MONEY, INNOCENT BLOOD, BLOOD OF THE LAMB, FLESH AND BLOOD.

Michael also writes historical hard-boiled thrillers, such as THE BIG GOODBYE, THE BIG BEYOND, and THE BIG HELLO featuring Jimmy "Soldier" Riley, a PI in Panama City during World War II. Ace Atkins calls the "Soldier" series "tough and violent with snappy dialogue and great atmosphere . . . a suspenseful, romantic and historic ride."

Michael Lister won his first Florida Book Award for his literary novel, DOUBLE EXPOSURE. His second Florida Book Award was for his fifth John Jordan novel BLOOD SACRIFICE.

Lister's latest literary thrillers include DOUBLE EXPOSURE, THUNDER BEACH, BURNT OFFERINGS, SEPARATION ANXIETY, and A CERTAIN RETRIBUTION.

His website is www.MichaelLister.com

Sign up for Michael's newsletter at his website and receive a free book. And don't forget to post a review of this and other books by Michael you've read.

CPSIA information can be obtained at www.ICGtesting.com
Printed in the USA
LVOW08s0825121014

408387LV00002B/86/P

9 781888 146462